Hidden

MIRIAM HALAHMY

Holiday House / New York

Many thanks to all of those fellow writers who have been so kind to comment on early drafts of this novel, in particular Tony Bradman who always gives such wise advice.

Derek Abra gave me the opportunity to view *Count Dracula*, one of the "little ships" that went to Dunkirk from Hayling.

Anqa Butt, Immigration and Legal Officer at the Medical Foundation for the Victims of Torture, gave valuable advice on immigration law and the plight of asylum seekers in Britain today.

To Anne Clark and Margot Edwards of the Anne Clark Agency, many thanks for bringing *Hidden* to America and to everyone at Holiday House, especially Mary Cash, huge thanks for taking our book and bringing it to the young people of the States.

Many thanks to all the Hayling Islanders who have always made me feel so welcome. When I cross Langstone Bridge from the mainland to the Island it is as though all the stresses of life slip away and the color blue spreads around me.

None of this would have been possible without the enduring and loyal support of my husband, Rafael, who shares my love of Hayling Island.

Library of Congress Cataloging-in-Publication Data

Names: Halahmy, Miriam, author.
Title: Hidden / Miriam Halahmy.
Description: First American edition. | New York : Holiday House, [2016] | "First published in Great Britain 2014 by Meadowside Books." | Summary: Fourteen-year-old Alix is faced with a huge moral dilemma when she helps pull an illegal Iraqi immigrant from the incoming tide on the coastal English island where she lives.
Identifiers: LCCN 2015050746 | ISBN 9780823436941 (hardcover)
Subjects: | CYAC: Family problems—Fiction. | Schools—Fiction. | Iraqis—England—Fiction. | Racism—Fiction. | Refugees—England—Fiction. | Immigrants—Fiction. | England—Fiction.
Classification: LCC PZ7.H12825 Hid 2016 | DDC [Fic]—dc23 LC record available at https://lccn.loc.gov/2015050746
ISBN: 978-0-8234-4026-9 (paperback)

For the Halahmy family,
who told me their stories of Iraq

Remember me when I am gone away,
Gone far away into the silent land;
When you can no more hold me by the hand...
From "Remember" by Christina Rossetti

Do not wrong a stranger or oppress him;
remember you were strangers in the land of Egypt.
Exodus 22:21

1. Hoodies on the High Street

School's out and I'm waiting for Kim when my phone bleeps. *Can't cum shppng. Gran sick. Soz.* So I'm stuck here on the High Street on my own, my best friend since forever sucked back into her superhuge family. I need a new top but I've got hardly any money left and Mum wants me home in one hour max, because since she broke her leg she expects me to do everything. Even clean the toilet.

"I'm not fifteen until May," I yelled at her earlier.

But she just said, "Save it. You'll find the bathroom cleaner under the sink."

"Might as well sell me into child slavery," I muttered, because since we've not been getting along, well not getting along even worse than usual because she broke her leg (which for the record wasn't my fault), it's just not worth winding her up. I try to think thoughts these days instead of actually saying them out loud, because you know how it is, everything you say out loud gets taken down and used as evidence, or recorded on cell phone and loaded onto YouTube, so everyone can view it. Well that's how it feels anyway.

I don't care about shopping anymore. It's not much fun by yourself. The shops are full of girls from school hanging out with their boyfriends and they're trying on the jewelry. Yes, the boys I mean, they're trying on the bracelets and stuff and the girls are screaming and laughing.

"Let's face it, Alix Miller," I say to myself, "you haven't even got a boyfriend." It's the Spring Rave on Saturday night at school and I've got no one to go with, again.

I pull my hair band out and drag my hair back more tightly, wishing I had enough money for one of those sparkly vests that look great with shorts and black tights. I walk back to the bus stop feeling completely miserable. When I get near, there's a crazy commotion just in front of me. Some boys are hooting and jeering. I can't make out what they're saying at first but as I get nearer I hear them yell, "Paki, Taliban, terrorist!"

I see Samir, the foreign boy from school. The hoodies have got him jammed up against a wall and they've begun chanting, "Paki out, Taliban out. Out, out, out!" They're really pushing their voices and shoving their arms like football hooligans.

People are crossing the street to avoid them and muttering into their shopping bags. The wind gusts all the takeout rubbish around our feet and whips back one of the gang's hoods from his head. I recognize Terrence, Lindy Bellows's big brother, who's a real thug, and a horrible feeling sinks into the pit of my stomach. No wonder Samir looks totally scared to bits. Samir's a bit taller than me and his black hair spikes up over his head making him look even more scared. He's wearing an Arsenal football scarf and his face is sort of pulled in as though he's trying to disappear.

Remember what I said about YouTube? All those thoughts that I try to keep in? Well, suddenly I'm shouting, "Leave him alone, pick on someone your own size!"

The gang turns and Terrence snarls, "Shut it, Alix! Unless you want some." God! He knows my name. Uh-oh! I'm in training for the Junior County Marathon, so I'm poised to sprint away when a police car pulls up, just like on the telly, and three ginormous cops in stab vests leap out.

The gang disappears in seconds and I see Samir's back whizzing off, Arsenal scarf flying out behind him. A tatty wallet slips out of his back pocket and onto the pavement.

The crowd that's gathered on the other side of the street trickle over the road, now that it's safe, and surround the police, saying how dangerous the High Street has become.

One of the policemen asks the crowd, "Did you recognize any of them?"

A woman in a see-through plastic mac shrieks out like a parrot, "Terrence Bellows!" and everyone says, "Yes, yes, that's him."

"Terrence Bellows has a police record. He isn't allowed anywhere in the town center." The policeman frowns.

The crowd snorts like a herd of bulls, but I've already picked up the wallet and I'm running after Samir who's dodged off down the next street. He's pretty slow, maybe a smoker, because I've almost caught him up when he comes to a halt, pulls out a key, lets himself into a flat beside a Chinese takeout and slams the door shut. I'm left standing out in the street, the smell of sweet-and-sour making me really hungry, wondering if I should knock on the door or just give up and go home. But the thought of Misery Guts Mum slouched in front of the telly giving out orders all evening overwhelms me, and without another thought I rap loudly on the door.

Nothing. I rap again a bit more halfheartedly.

A Chinese woman comes out of the takeout and says, "Do bell, they not hear you." She has a tired, wrinkly sort of face and she's wearing bright red slippers on her feet. When I look

3

at the door again I can see a grubby bell with the wires hanging out of the side.

I press the bell and it rings somewhere above me and then I hear the thunder of feet coming down a long staircase. Someone rattles a chain and the door opens a sort of cautious crack. It's Samir and when he sees me he stares at me and I stare back.

"Girlfriend visit you," the Chinese lady pipes up and she lets out a peal of shrill laughter, which echoes around the street.

I feel my face go bright red and the door slams shut. More chain rattling, the door opens wide and, frowning at the Chinese lady, Samir says, "Come in."

I hesitate, thinking, Should I? What would Mum say? and even, What if they are terrorists? But then I think that's so crazy that I run up the stairs after Samir.

The smell of Chinese food fades and it's replaced with a strange smell, which I completely don't recognize. Samir pushes open a door and leads the way into the kitchen. It's very small and every surface is covered in cooking stuff: mixing bowls, wooden spoons and huge metal baking trays all smeared with a sticky-looking mixture.

I'm just wondering what it is when Samir says, "Auntie Selma's been making baklava."

For once I keep my mouth shut and just think in silence, Why does his auntie make balaclavas? Aren't they like ski masks that terrorists wear, and anyhow why would she make them in the kitchen while she's baking?

4

2. Suspicions

"Is this yours?" I ask, holding out the wallet.

Samir nods in a shy sort of way and mutters, "Thank you." He puts the wallet in his pocket.

I don't know what else to say. Samir only joined our class this term and I don't really know him. I'm just wondering where he's from and if I should ask when the door below us slams shut and footsteps echo on the stairs. Samir throws me a nervous look and I'm thinking, Is it too late to hide? when Samir-mark-II appears in the doorway. Same black hair, not quite so spiky, same dark eyes and dark skin but quite a bit taller and a few years older.

"This is Naazim, my brother," says Samir.

Naazim fixes me with a suspicious stare and I can't help thinking that if anyone looks like a terrorist, he does. He has this sort of smoldering look on his face you see on suspected bombers they show on TV and he's wearing very greasy overalls. Car mechanic, I decide. But fortunately I manage to keep silent.

Naazim barks out, "Who you are?"

He has a strong accent and I'm wondering if he's from Pakistan or maybe Afghanistan, when he snaps, "Where you live?"

I glance over at Samir for support but he's fixed on his

brother so I shrug and start to explain about the gang. But then Samir catches my eye and something in his look makes me stop. He doesn't want Naazim to know about the bullies on the high street and his dark eyes have such a pleading look that I pull up short and instead mutter, "I'm Alix. I live on Hayling Island."

Naazim's face gets even darker and he starts rattling away to Samir in this totally foreign language. His voice is rising as he waves his hand about, which is also covered with grease, and he keeps shooting me poisonous looks. He's standing between me and the door so there's no way out and Samir can't get a word in edgewise. It's starting to get scary and I try to gauge whether I could slip past and race down the stairs. I can't help wondering if they go on like this all the time. Maybe they're planning their next attack on mainland Britain. The battery in my useless cell phone is probably too flat to call the police.

Naazim keeps going like a rocket and in the end I'm getting so tense I start to fiddle about with some lemon peel lying around on the counter. There's nothing I can do until Naazim lets me go, assuming of course that he will, and I'm just wondering what I should do if he doesn't when Samir says in English, "She's just leaving."

It's then I realize the difference.

Samir speaks really good English, with hardly any accent. In the end Naazim just grunts, "Samir must clean kitchen," and he's gone, leaving us alone.

I'm so relieved I let out a big sigh and throw Samir a look, expecting him to say something like, "Big brothers, what a waste of space." But he just stands there staring toward the door. I've never seen anyone keep so still.

It feels quite weird so I say, "I'd better go."

Samir nods and I follow him back downstairs again, but as

I go out the front door he calls out, "See you in school?" He has that sort of lost, pleading look in his eyes again, so I call back, "Okay," and sprint off to the bus stop, but I can't help feeling relieved I'm outside again.

Families can be so embarrassing, I think as the bus pulls out of town. I don't blame Samir for not spilling anything to his brother. Maybe Naazim is a bit of a bully himself.

I'm just deciding that Samir is the best at English in his family, that they all rely on him and so he doesn't want to tell them about the bullies and look weak in front of his brother, when someone halfway down the bus says out loud to no one in particular, "They want their heads examinined."

I whip around in shock. What do they know?

Then I see Mrs. Saddler from our street nodding toward a windsurfer tacking across the choppy sea out in Langstone Harbor. I should have guessed. Mrs. Saddler's always complaining about something. Last week she told Mum I shouldn't be running around on the beach anymore. "She doesn't keep that dog of hers under proper control. I wouldn't let my Jeremy run about on the yacht club road unleashed."

She's such an old bat. She hasn't got a clue what I have to do to train for the marathon, and my dog, Trudy, loves to run with me, her daft spaniel ears flopping from side to side. Jeremy couldn't run to save his life.

My phone rings. It's Kim. Finally!

"Gran's okay," she says. To be honest I'd completely forgotten all about our shopping trip and why it was canceled. "So Mum's happy. She was really worried," Kim goes on.

"Great," I say, but I can't help feeling a bit jealous.

Kim has sisters, brothers, a mum and a dad, and that's just for starters. My dad skipped two years ago. Disappeared with

Gorgeous Gloria—Mum and me call her the Gremlin—and we haven't heard from him since. We moved into Grandpa's little cottage when Dad left but then Grandpa died last year and now it's just us two. And the broken leg of course.

My phone crackles and I say to Kim, "You'll never guess where I've been."

"Where?" she says.

"A suicide bomber's house!" I say.

3. Elephants

"Tell me everything," gasps Kim.

Mrs. Saddler's pushing off the bus in front of me so I say, "I'll ring you later," and click off.

Back home Mum starts the minute I get in. "Alexandra?" she yells from her usual position in front of the telly and she's using the name.

"It's Alix with an *i*," I yell back. But she never listens. I'm named after Grandma so she refuses to shorten it.

"The supermarket delivery came," Mum goes on. "I expected you hours ago."

She sounds really grumpy; she's probably been sitting watching the clock all afternoon.

I'm actually thirty-four minutes early but there's no point arguing.

Mum's been ordering the shopping online since she can't drive with her broken leg. It happened when she got out of bed. She was just getting up and somehow she tripped and bam! By the time the ambulance came, I thought she might die just from screaming. It's quite a bad break and she's no good on crutches. She might even lose her office job, which is only temporary anyway.

I took on a newspaper route, even though I've got loads of

course work. Well, we've got to eat, haven't we? And Dad's not doing anything to help.

I put my head around the living room door and nearly faint from the heat. The log-effect gas fire is roaring and the room smells from dirty plates and apple cores on the coffee table. Mum's lounging around as usual with her leg up on the footstool.

Mum still sleeps in the living room, which is quite handy now she's broken her leg. Our cottage only has two bedrooms. I have the little one at the back, overlooking the sea. Mum has a bed, which turns into a sofa in the day, and she keeps all her clothes in my wardrobe. Of course she could move into the big front bedroom now that Grandpa has died, but she doesn't want to.

"When I'm ready," she keeps saying, and now of course that'll be months.

She could try a bit harder with the crutches, though, couldn't she, I think now as I glare at her from the doorway. She's wearing her baggiest jeans that she's ripped up the left side because of the plaster, but she's put safety pins all along the rip.

Mum was a punk when she was younger. She had the only Mohawk on Hayling Island. Green and pink. Tragic. But when she met Dad he made her shave it off. She still wears sort of punk fashion, with safety pins in her jeans and thick black boots, even though she's forty-one and beginning to go gray at the sides. "Joe Strummer's older than me," she always says when I point out a gray hair.

He's in the seventies punk band, The Clash, and actually, the music's pretty cool.

She's into spoken-word poetry and stuff like that. Before Dad left and Grandpa died she went out every Wednesday night reading out her poetry in pubs. I went to see her once. Dad refused, said he wanted to watch something on the telly, but now I think he went out with the Gremlin. Mum looked really good, with blond highlights in her hair, which is darker than mine, and kohl around her eyes and her arty nail polish. They all clapped and cheered when she finished. I felt quite proud and she let me have a sip of her beer when the bartender wasn't looking.

But she seems to have forgotten all about that since she broke her leg.

"Everyone calls me Alix, even Grandpa did," I grumble to her now.

But Mum ignores it. "Just sort out the shopping," she snaps, "we'll have rolls and cheese for supper. My leg's been killing me all morning."

Another boring sandwich, I think, but she hears me. I forgot to flip the silent switch.

"Sor-ry," she shrieks. "I can't help not being a superstar TV chef!"

Kim's dad is a chef at a big hotel in Portsmouth. He makes the best steak and chips in the universe. And he makes sticky toffee pudding.

Mum grapples for the remote control and switches channels. As I go back to the kitchen I can hear the raucous laughter of some quiz show pouring through the cottage. I hate those programs.

Trudy's looking up at me with her gorgeous spaniel eyes, puzzled at the loud voices, and I whisper to her, "I have to do everything around here, it's so not fair." I bury my face in her soft coat and wonder how things got so bad. I never used to think about stuff like I do now.

Trudy starts to lick my face and it calms me like always. I give myself a proper doggy shake and then start sorting out the shopping. I'm putting the cans in the cupboard wondering where all this food comes from and I find myself thinking about Samir again. He can't have been born here, can he? Because his brother doesn't speak good English.

Then I pick up a packet of coffee and look at the label. I've never even thought about this before but did you know that coffee comes from Kenya? And the sugar's from Malawi. It's Fair Trade, which I think is meant to be good. There's a useful fact on the packet: Elephants run at 25 mph.

My top speed is 6 mph and I've only seen elephants in the zoo. Must be amazing seeing them out your bedroom window if you live in Africa. Maybe Samir used to ride elephants in his country, although he's not black, so is he from India?

I wander back into the living room holding the sugar packet and say to Mum, "Do they have elephants in India as well as Africa?"

But you know how with adults if you choose the wrong moment? Her face wrinkles with rage and she huffs, "I missed that answer! Can't you get on by yourself for one minute?!"

I feel like my blood is about to boil over. It's been a totally worthless day and now Mum hits the roof because I ask her a question about elephants!

So I yell back, "Didn't you know slavery was abolished two hundred years ago?!" Grabbing Trudy's leash I rip my coat off the peg and I'm down the path in a nanosecond, the front door slamming so hard it practically takes the windows out.

"I'm fed up!" I yell. Trudy looks at me but I don't care who else is listening. Some of the neighbors are out in their gardens in the houses opposite, nattering over the fences, but they don't hear. They think I'm just a stupid kid anyway.

Better face up to it, Alix, I moan to myself as we tear down the yacht club road to the beach, you're on your own now. Mum's gone into free fall, hanging on to me like her parachute just failed; Grandpa's dead—God, I hate that word—and I've got to give up my silly baby fantasies that Dad's going to turn up bored with the Gremlin, begging us to take him back. He never even rings. Who's going to look after me? I can't even relight the boiler when it blows out in an east wind. "It's coming straight from Siberia," Grandpa used to say. He was a sailor and knew about winds. He also knew how to look after us.

We head past the Lifeboat Station and down onto the beach. When the tide goes out you can run for miles on the sand and I know everyone is supposed to worship the sun but summer just makes me hot and sweaty. I prefer winter. On gray days like today you can hardly see where the beach stops and the sea begins.

There's only about fifteen minutes of daylight left but there are still a few boats out on the sea. Their lights coming on like lonely fireflies make me feel even more miserable. I can't be bothered to run with Trudy anymore, so I just wander down to the old concrete pillbox. Sometimes teenagers hang around here, drinking beer and lighting fires on the beach when it gets dark. I've seen Lindy Bellows here with her brother and his gang, smoking joints probably. I keep well away.

But today it just stinks of wee.

Then my phone goes. I wrench it from my jacket pocket. It's Kim.

"Suicide bomber?" she squeals down the phone and for a second I can't think what she means.

Then I remember and start to tell her about Samir being bullied by the hoodies and my suspicions about Naazim and I must admit they sound really silly when I say them out loud.

"But did you actually see anything, like sticks of dynamite?" Kim says, beginning to laugh.

"Well no," I say.

"Or videos of Osama Bin Laden hidden down the back of the sofa?"

She's really warming up now and, of course, she's my best friend so she knows me really well.

"Honest, Ali, you're such a drama queen, Samir's just some nobody in our year and Naazim is his boring brother."

Kim always tries to keep my feet on the ground. She's usually the one who stops me when I go into a real fury.

"Samir's all right. He's got nice eyes," I say without thinking. There's a pause and I'm wondering if the signal's gone. Then Kim says, "Well, if you like that sort of thing."

If you like that sort of thing? What does she mean?

4. Two Percent

It's freezing next morning and the February wind is slicing through my jacket as I arrive at school. Everyone's hurrying toward the gates, desperate to get inside. Our school is always boiling hot. In summer the sun fries us through the enormous windows and in winter the heaters blow out stinking hot air.

It's already late and I'm about to sprint forward when I spot Samir near the gates. A couple of Year 11 boys with rugby shoulders bursting out of their blazers overtake me and I see one of them grab Samir, shove him to one side and snarl, "Out my way, Paki."

There's a hard, almost metal smell in the air and the sky is elephant gray.

Why haven't I noticed this stuff before? But the school buzzer is drilling into my head and if I'm late again Mr. Spicer, our form teacher, will give me detention so I jog forward and call out to Samir as I pass him.

"You coming?"

Samir straightens and stares at me and I can't help noticing that his nose is very broad with flared nostrils and he has dark stubble showing on his upper lip. It makes him look much older than fourteen.

Then his face breaks into a wonderful smile and for the first time he looks normal, not like some miserable kid everyone's always picking on.

"All right," he says.

We fall into step but Samir's gone all silent again, so I say, "Saturday tomorrow." He nods but he doesn't say anything, so I ask casually, "What do you do on the weekends?"

Samir just shrugs. He looks like he's shrinking back into himself and without really thinking, I say, "Come down to Hayling sometime."

"Okay," he says.

He gives me a look as if to say, Do you really mean it?, which makes me wonder if I really do. So then I feel guilty and as we arrive at the classroom door I say, "Come tomorrow morning if you want, we can walk my dog on the beach."

Kim's already at our table, Mozart score open, and I can see she's practicing her fingering on an imaginary clarinet, totally in her own world. Sometimes I think she's in love with Mozart.

But Lindy Bellows, that's right, Terrence's sister, sees me and Samir chatting and calls out, "Must be desperate for a kiss to go with him."

There's a general sniggering around the class and I feel myself going all red. Samir slinks off into his usual seat alone at the back.

What's it got to do with her? I think, and I feel myself flare up again, like with Mum over the shopping. It seems to happen so quickly these days.

Grandpa used to say, "Choose your battles, Alix," so I just sit down as Mr. Spicer sweeps in. He dresses like a bank manager, black suits, white shirts, and he slicks his yucky brown hair down with gel.

Spicer barks out the class register in his high-pitched voice like an overexcited terrier. Lindy's name is first. She doesn't answer but he just ignores her. All the teachers do. She frightens them. She's about as mean as you can get, she's got frizzy ginger hair and she keeps the nail on her right forefinger sharpened to a spear and she was arrested for shoplifting just before Christmas. Her brothers are always in and out of jail. Everyone knows the Bellows family. Me and Kim keep well clear.

Our first lesson is Citizenship with Mr. Spicer and he announces we're doing Immigration. I perk up; this could be useful. Maybe I'll find out where Samir and Naazim come from. I glance over at Kim but she's got the Mozart score on her lap and she's tapping her fingers up and down her right leg.

Spicer says he's going to start with the facts and a groan goes up around the class. He can be dead boring once he starts but this time I try to listen.

"Who can tell me the definition of an immigrant?" He looks around the class. No one says anything. He starts to jig up and down on his heels. He can be *so* irritating. I think he's going to keep us waiting until the bell goes.

Then he says, "Immigrants are people who go and live permanently in another country. It's important to understand that people leave their countries for different reasons."

Okay, I think, so maybe I'll find out the reason Samir is here. I lean over to whisper to Kim but she's still finger tapping on her knee.

"One group of immigrants are called economic migrants," says Spicer. "These are people who have the right to live and work here, people who have moved for economic reasons."

"Like all those Polish plumbers?" says one of the Science Club geeks.

"Exactly," says Spicer, looking pleased.

Someone yawns rudely and Spicer glares around the class. Everyone goes very quiet. Spicer hands out detentions with lightning speed. He starts droning on again about the EU and I drift off thinking about the weekend.

Then he says, "Another group of immigrants are refugees," and I tune in again. This could be useful.

"There are a lot of myths and stories on TV and in the papers about refugees," says Spicer. "It's important you know the facts, right?"

No one says anything. Are they even listening? I decide to nod in the teacher's direction but he doesn't even notice me. So nothing new there.

"Now," says Spicer, and he picks up a leaflet. I can hear a few subdued sighs behind me. "According to the UN," he goes on, waving the leaflet in the air, "refugees are people who have a 'well-founded fear of persecution or death in their own countries.' When they arrive in the UK they have to say they are 'seeking asylum,' which means protection from our government."

"Like all them Romanians," someone calls out in a nasty tone.

I jerk my head around but I can't see who it is. I look back at Mr. Spicer, he doesn't seem too worried.

"No, Romanians have the right to come and work here, they're not refugees," he says.

"What's the difference?" asks one of the science geeks. Lindy gives a loud yawn but Spicer ignores her. "Romania is in the EU, like Britain, and so we can live and work in each other's countries. Refugees are people who are fleeing their countries because they are threatened with unfair imprisonment, torture or death."

"Yeah, well my dad says all them asylum seekers are bogus. It's in the papers. We should chuck 'em out," calls out Charlie Parks.

Some people mutter in agreement and I turn around to glare at him.

Charlie bares his teeth at me. He's such a bully. He's a starter on the football team and built like a tank. So I just toss my head and turn back but my insides do a flip.

"My dad says they're all thieves anyway. They take our jobs and our houses."

That's Jess Jayne, from the Jayne family. There's three of them. They're not really sisters but the meanest girl gang in the school. They speak posh and they're from minted families so the teachers like them. They all added Jayne to their first names because one of them is called Sarah Jane. Only they spell it with a *y*. Very clever, I don't think.

Jess and Charlie have really set things off. People start shouting horrible comments just like the sort of thing I heard on the street against Samir. I twist around to try and catch his eye but he's hunched over his desk, his face buried in his arms. Somebody says, "That's racist," and then the noise in the classroom starts to rise as people start arguing.

I give Kim another nudge.

"What?" she says, and I can see she hasn't been listening. Her head is full of Mozart. Doesn't she care about this stuff? "All right you lot, settle down," yells Mr. Spicer, and the room goes gradually quiet. "Let's get one thing straight. There's no such thing as a 'bogus asylum seeker.' All refugees have the right to ask for asylum under international law."

"Even if they're all terrorists," says Charlie with a smirk.

Jess lets out a silly scream and the Jayne family laugh, but Mr. Spicer silences them with another glare.

"Show some respect, Year 10," snaps Mr. Spicer, and he glares around the class. The room goes silent. "In Britain, not everyone is granted asylum," he goes on. "They have to prove their case to the Home Office and believe me, it's very, very difficult. They need a top-notch lawyer. Sometimes they wait for years for their case to be decided and all that time they live in fear of being deported, sent back to their own country where they could be tortured or even put to death."

He stops and looks around the room but no one says anything. "All they might have done is say their prime minister is stupid."

"They say that on the news every day here," someone calls out.

"Exactly," says Mr. Spicer.

"So what happens if no one believes them?" asks the science geek.

"If they fail to convince the authorities that they've run away from danger then they can be sent home. But once their story is accepted they stop being asylum seekers and they get refugee status, accepted as refugees. They can work and they won't be deported, which would come as a huge relief as I'm sure you can imagine."

Some people nod and there's more muttering. Then the science geek says, "What about illegal immigrants, you hear about them all the time."

"Good question," says Spicer, and Charlie gives a sarcastic snort. "Some people try to come in illegally, hiding out in trucks and on boats. If they're discovered and not in fear of persecution, they're deported straightaway. But sometimes they're genuine refugees in desperate need of asylum and their stories have simply not been believed. It's a very complicated picture. Put yourselves in their shoes for a minute."

While we all think about this he thumps keys for the interactive white board. A number comes up—9.2 million.

"That's approximately how many refugees there are in the world today," he says, straightening his tie with such a smug smile I almost wish he was wrong. Then he taps out another number—2.7 percent.

"That's the percentage of the world's refugees who make it to the UK. The other 97.3 percent go somewhere else."

"Two percent too many," sneers Lindy. Mr. Spicer ignores her.

"And they're not all terrorists, Charlie Parks."

People mutter but Lindy's voice grates over them, "Yeah? Prove it."

She's got her mouth slightly open and her tongue stuck in her cheek as if to say, You can't, can you? She's twirling a broken pencil between her fingers.

Spicer doesn't say anything. Why doesn't he stand up to her? Kim isn't even listening. It feels like I always have to do everything on my own these days. I don't have any facts and figures at my fingertips, except the speed at which elephants run.

And I can't quote my dad because he never had opinions about anything except why he kept losing his jobs, which was always the boss's fault of course or the useless computer networks. He did have one opinion—about punks. "Neanderthal throwbacks," he'd mutter whenever Mum spiked her hair or laced up her Doc Martens.

That was one of the problems between Mum and Dad. He didn't appreciate her being a punk, Mum always said. Even

21

though she shaved off her Mohawk when they got married. "Love's not enough," she'd say. Dad was always trying to change her right from the beginning.

But I miss my dad.

Spicer's droning on about how immigrants have contributed a lot to this country and then Lindy says in a sarcastic voice, "Like what?"

"Like fish and chips," he snaps back, and a laugh goes around the class.

That's told her, I think, and I try to catch Kim's eye. But she's staring at her music score under the desk.

"Around eighteen Nobel prizes have been won by refugees," Spicer goes on. He's really warming up now, listing painters, writers and musicians. I'm impressed and I can see some of the others are too.

But then he starts on statistics again, arms folded, eyes fixed on the back wall and I find it harder to concentrate.

Someone says something behind me again, but I'm not really listening until Spicer replies in a dramatic voice, "Never forget, many of these people we're talking about are fleeing war, torture, illegal imprisonment, death."

Someone snorts and scrapes back his chair. Spicer stops and puts his hands on his hips with a warning look. No one speaks.

I crick my neck around to catch Samir's eye but he's still slumped down on his desk. Did he come to England to escape torture or death? A chill scutters down my spine.

"So not all refugees are here illegally," Spicer goes on in a stern voice. "Many of them have come here because otherwise they'd be dead or frankly worse." Worse? So what could be worse than death? I think.

I'm just about to call out when the door flings open and the student teacher from next door rushes in, sobbing.

You can see that Mr. Spicer enjoys being Buzz Lightyear, saving the day.

He mutters something to the student teacher, then says to us with a glare, "Read pages 91 through 95 and answer the questions. I'm just going next door with Miss Redding. I expect total silence," and he's gone.

The class is quiet for a second and then Lindy swivels around in her chair, points her spear nail directly at Samir and snarls, "Two percent too many."

5. Pants

Seven o'clock Saturday morning I go out to do my paper route and I can't see my hand in front of my face. A dense sea mist is covering our end of the Island. No one's out, not even Mrs. Saddler with Jeremy. She'll probably just chuck him in the back garden today. Me and Trudy run on the beach whatever.

My marathon trainer says running on sand will strengthen my muscles. He thinks I could win. I really, really want to win because you get interviewed by the papers. I've already decided what I'm going to say and I know it's completely insane but it could be my one and only hope.

Dad, if you're reading this then you know I've won the Junior County Marathon but it's not worth it unless you come home or at least ring me.

How else am I going to find him? Mum never talks about him so I have to try and find him myself.

I'll give them my cell phone number to print in case he's lost it.

It's freezing and my hands inside my thermal mountain gloves are already numb. I'll probably die from frostbite. Can it actually kill you or is it just that your fingers drop off? Would that be worse than death?

I had asked Kim what she thought would be worse.

"Never hearing Mozart again," she'd said, still running her fingers over her legs, and that was in the lunch queue.

She was really strange yesterday. I was shooting baskets with Samir after lunch. He's always on his own and anyway he's sort of nice, quieter than the other boys. Once we started, a couple of other kids joined in and then I saw Kim on the other side of the playground. I called out to her but she just ignored me.

What was that all about?

I didn't get another chance to ask her. We were in different classes in the afternoon and then she disappeared off to band practice straight after school.

I shift the cart with the newspapers into my other hand and start to jog to try and keep warm. The foghorns are moaning out on the Solent, that's the bit of sea between Hayling and the Isle of Wight where Grandpa was going to teach me to sail, only then he died. The shrouds are jingling and rattling away on the boats down at the yacht club. They make me feel a bit like one of those old sailors navigating the streets in the fog, wondering if I'll fall off the edge of the flat world.

By the time I make it back to the newspaper store I'm a total block of ice.

Chaz hands me a mug of coffee. "You're a proper little star, Alix. Cold as a monkey's bum out there, wouldn't catch no London kids out on a morning like this."

Chaz looks a bit like a jockey, small and thin and sort of wired up all the time. He's always dashing around the shop, straightening the papers, filling up the cold cabinet. He's got very pale skin, with red blotches on his face. His hair is short and mouse brown and he combs it back all the time with a plastic comb he keeps in his shirt pocket.

"Bet it's warmer in London," I grumble, almost burning my numb fingers off on the hot mug.

But Chaz loves the Island. He tells everyone, "Wouldn't never live nowhere else now."

I'm so cold I sprint all the way home and throw myself down in the living room with Trudy on my lap and the log-effect gas fire up full.

I'm sort of dozing when I hear a crash and a loud scream. Oh my God! Mum! I rush in the kitchen and find the teapot in pieces on the floor and Mum running her hand under the cold tap. "Burned myself," she says in a wobbly voice.

I can't even doze without her winding me up, so I go upstairs to finish my homework.

By midday Mum is already comatose in front of the telly. I swear I nearly got out Grandpa's ladder last night to climb onto the roof and knock down the aerial. Only the thought of having to talk to Mum all day actually stopped me.

"Walk," I say to Trudy, and she jumps up with a little bark of delight.

I leap the stairs in two halves, it's only a small cottage, and clip her leash on before she goes completely mad, crashing into the front door.

"Just off to the beach," I call out.

No answer. Mum's still asleep. Excellent.

Out in the street the sea mist is worse if that's possible. I can't even see Mrs. Saddler's house across the road but I can smell the wood smoke from her fire. That's one of my favorite smells, up there with lemon peel and Prada perfume, which Kim gave me last Christmas and makes me feel, well, really sexy when I wear it and we go out to a club.

We're really too young to get into clubs and Kim is really

small, she only comes up to my chin, but she has long dark brown hair with these amazing red lights in it and under the strobes they sort of glitter. I'm almost five six, which is great for running, but I'm too skinny, not really pretty or attractive like Kim.

At New Year's, Jaxie, Kim's big sister, who's eighteen and works weekends in a club in Portsmouth, got us in for free. It was awesome. Kim was seriously worried about someone spiking our drinks; we only drank Budweiser from the bottle. She worries about everything. Even crossing the road at traffic lights. We danced with two of the 12th-year boys and even made out. Maybe they'll be at the Spring Rave tonight. Kim managed to rip herself away from Mozart long enough yesterday to say, "Yes, of course we're still going."

Down the yacht club road the sea mist is so thick I can't see the clubhouse at the end of the point. There's a salty seaweed smell in the air and a lot of rubbish has washed up overnight onto the main beach on the Solent side.

The tide is in and the water is very choppy. It's that cold gray color that makes you shiver just to look at it.

It's getting colder, if that's possible, and even *I* don't think it's safe to run in this.

Trudy's already looking up at me as if to say, Isn't it lunchtime yet?

Why do dogs only think about food?

Why do mums and dads, well my mum and dad, only think about themselves? Then I have the thought I've had so many times before, I'm sick of it. Why did Dad disappear off the face of the earth? He could've kept in touch with me at least. It's not as if he's a spy and switched sides, or lost his memory or become an astronaut. It didn't always used to be like this. Dad and I used to do loads of stuff like go bowling. When we got to the bowling alley, we'd put on our special shoes, then we'd always talk American. We'd say things like Mom and fries and cookies and pants.

Dad would say, "Hey, Alix, pull your pants up," or I'd say, "Hey, Dad, I need some new pants!" and everyone would turn around and stare and expect to see me wearing my underpants over my jeans. We'd both scream with laughter.

Then a familiar voice thuds me back to the real world. "Hi, Alix."

It's Samir, emerging from the mist like a ghost.

6. Into the Sea

Did you know that elephants weigh up to six thousand kilograms and yet they pad about so silently you don't know they're coming until they've practically crushed you to death? Well, Samir appeared like an elephant.

"Where did you spring from?" I snap, feeling spooked.

"I came on the bus," he says. He looks half frozen, hunched in his gray sweatshirt and denim jacket, his hands stuffed in his pockets. "Is this where you live?"

Then I remember I'd invited him and feel a bit mean, snapping like that.

"Yes, over there." I nod in the direction of our cottage.

"I never know what to do on Saturdays," says Samir, kicking through some of the rubbish on the beach.

"I'm just walking my dog, you can hang out if you want," I say, and his face relaxes into that terrific smile. I want to tell him he should flash that around in school a bit more. It makes him look taller and less of a frightened rabbit.

But instead I say, "Your brother's a bit fierce." Samir sort of tucks into himself and I don't want him to think I'm being rude so I say quickly, "Families, who'd have them."

Samir just stands there staring out to sea and I wonder how

he manages to keep everything to himself. Not like me, always blurting stuff out.

I'm just about to suggest hot chocolate back at my house when we hear the sound of a motorboat coming straight toward us across the sea lane. The mist is still quite thick so we can't actually see it and I'm thinking that it's a bit dangerous out there today. I haven't seen any other boats going out.

The engine roars as someone pulls the throttle back and there's a lot of shouting and then we hear a single scream and a massive splash. It sounds as if someone is dumping a fridge or something at sea and then a gap appears in the mist.

I can't believe my eyes!

"There's a man in the water!" I yell. I look around desperately for some help, but there's nobody except Samir. Trudy has started to bark as I run down the pebbly slope to the beach, thoughts flying through my mind. The water's freezing and the currents here are so strong they could drag him under. He's going to have to start swimming or he'll drown. As I get to the water's edge, I look around at the Lifeboat Station. It looms up through the mist but I didn't see anyone over there earlier. I look back at the sea just as a huge wave breaks over the man's head and he disappears. Oh God! There's no time to raise the alarm. The currents will drag him under. I have to go in and get him. Why is this happening to me?

Then I see his head break the surface and I stop in relief, waiting for him to start swimming. But all he does is scream out and splash around, gasping for air. Another wave breaks over his head and he disappears again under the surface.

Samir has run up and I can hear him breathing hard behind me. This is the most dangerous water around Hayling Island, all eddies and currents and whirlpools.

"Never go swimming by the yacht club," Grandpa said, almost every day. "You'll be swept out to sea and drown. No one will save you." It used to make chills run down my spine.

I never even paddle here. But I don't have a choice now, I can't leave this man to drown. Grandpa wouldn't, would he? I throw off my jacket and kick off my shoes and I'm not sure if I'm trembling from cold or terror.

"I'll have to go in," I yell to Samir. "Stay here, the currents are very strong."

Then I'm in the sea and it's so cold my throat seizes up. I'm up to my knees almost immediately and I know if it gets to my chest I won't be able to breathe. The man surfaces, flailing about. Just a few more steps and I'm praying to God and elephants and everything else that I don't get swept away and Mum has to make her own dinner tonight.

The water is up to my waist. I can feel the beach dropping away sharply and the current is beginning to suck at my feet. I can't go much farther. I lean forward and fling out my arms but he's just out of reach. His eyes are wild with fear and his arms are flailing out in all directions. I take another step forward but I can't feel anything beneath my feet and I jerk back, nearly falling down. The man screams and reaches toward me, just as a huge wave splashes my face, blinding me for a few seconds. When my eyes clear I can see the man is a bit nearer. It's now or never, I think, and straining forward I manage to grab his wrist. He's so slippery and heavy I almost let go, but Samir is in the water now and reaches us just in time. Together we heave the man back up to dry land and collapse on the ground.

I'm lying there practically dead myself and Trudy is whimpering and licking my face and then I hear Samir gasp. I open my eyes. It's like a horror film.

I'm practically eyeball to eyeball with the man and his face is all bloody and bruised, one eye puffed up like a football. Terrified, I scrabble backward and grip Trudy to my chest so hard she yelps in pain.

"Is he dead?" I whisper, my teeth already beginning to chatter violently from the cold.

Samir doesn't answer. He's up on his knees, his fingers on the man's wrist, looking for a pulse. If he's not dead, I think, he will be soon. This bloke didn't have time to get dressed this morning. He's only wearing a pair of tatty shorts. Trudy escapes from my arms and starts to lick the man's face, which seems a good idea, and then there's a spluttering sound and Samir props up the lifeless-looking head, pushing Trudy away.

I know I should try and rub some life into his blue-looking legs. Grandpa was always going on about sailors practically freezing to death at sea. "Hypothermia. The body temperature drops quick on deck in winter," he used to say, scanning the horizon.

But I can't bring myself to touch the creepy flesh. Maybe he's already dead, I think, and this is what they mean in books by being in "death throes."

I grab Trudy's collar and pull her away. A weird sound like shouting under water comes from the man's mouth and he opens his one good eye and some water dribbles from the corner of his mouth. Don't be sick, I plead silently. I'm no good if someone's sick.

But the man isn't sick, instead a torrent of words pours out of his mouth, at first in a very croaky voice and then louder and louder, until he's shouting like a lunatic and throwing his arms around.

Trouble is I can't understand a word.

7. No Hiding Place

Trudy is straining on her leash and whining while the man rages on and then suddenly Samir starts speaking. I can't understand a word he's saying either.

"Hey!" I call out, which is really hard because my teeth are chattering like a road drill. "What's he saying?" It feels as though my brain has turned to ice. Maybe I'm scrambling up everything I hear.

But they both ignore me and then just as suddenly they stop. Samir stands up, his head and shoulders slumped.

"Samir, w-w-w-what's going on?" I say.

Samir just turns and walks to the water's edge, not noticing how his shabby sneakers begin to get soaked again. I stand up too, looking down at the man. He's closed his good eye and his whole body is shaking with cold. He won't last much longer out here. We can't carry him to the cottage and I can't run around and get Mum with the car because of her broken leg.

"We have to call an ambulance."

Samir doesn't move a muscle. He stands silently staring out to sea. Is he mad? "Samir, he'll die out here," I say. "It's freezing!"

I'm pulling on my coat and sneakers as I speak. My fingers are too numb to tie the laces and I can't even do the zip on my jacket. Samir has wrapped his denim jacket around the man's shaking shoulders, but he still doesn't seem to get it.

"Samir!" I say firmly, but he still ignores me. "I'm going home to phone for help."

"No!" Samir turns and yells at me. Then he's running back over the beach, his sneakers squelching. He catches his foot in a trail of heavy seaweed and, stopping to untangle it, he calls out in a softer voice, "No ambulance, no police, you mustn't even tell your mother."

My mother? Why not? But I find myself staring into Samir's eyes and there's that pleading look again, tugging away at me like the currents.

I shake my head to clear it and say furiously, "What are you going on about? He is going to get hypothermia!"

"Yes, yes, I know, he's really cold and he hasn't eaten for three days..."

"How do you know? He can't even speak clearly."

"Because he speaks my language: Arabic. Alix, he is an illegal immigrant, like Mr. Spicer talked about in class yesterday. He is here without permission." Samir's voice drops to a whisper as he says these last words and he looks nervously around in case someone's listening.

Arabic! Samir and Naazim are from some Arab country and so is this stranger.

It's very hard to think straight with my brain shuddering and my teeth chattering and my whole body shaking with cold.

"What do you mean? Why is he here and why on earth did he jump into the sea on a day like this? He could have been killed or worse." *Worse,* there's that word again.

I start to run up the sand dune to see if anyone else is around. What would I say if one of the neighbors went past right now?

Samir is calling up to me in a really desperate voice. "We have to help him. He's run away from his country because they wanted to kill him, you know, like Mr. Spicer told us. He's an asylum seeker, only in his case the government, the Home Office, they refused him. So he's an illegal immigrant...," and his voice fades away.

Illegal. Oh God, and then I remember Lindy's mocking voice, "Two percent too many." She doesn't even think Samir should be here, what would she say about our drowning man?

"We have to help him," pleads Samir. "His name's Mohammed and he's hurt. He was tortured..."

"What?"

"Tortured, like my..." But he doesn't finish. His eyes cloud over as he looks up at me.

"Help me to hide him, Alix. Please. Just for a couple of days."

Hide him? Hide a stranger? I look back down to where the man is lying all scrunched up on the sand, his body shaking and twitching. His face has gone a deathly pale and his lips are literally blue. The bruised eye looks so swollen; someone must have really punched him hard. What did he do to deserve that? My feet feel as though they are sinking into the sand, and soon my whole body will be stuck fast like in a swamp and I won't be able to run away even if I want to.

"Alix, we don't have much time, someone will come." Samir's voice breaks into my thoughts. The man is groaning and shaking and Samir is pleading and the mist is clearing quite quickly now. We'll be discovered very soon or our man will die of the cold. What should I do?

The man is shivering worse than ever. I have to make a decision. "We have to get him to the hospital, let's get him to the bus stop, okay?" I say.

"No, we can't! You don't understand!" says Samir, and he's sounding completely desperate. "He's here illegally and the hospital will tell the police and then he could get deported straightaway. Trust me, Alix, we have to hide him, now!"

"But surely they've only got to look at him," I say.

"And what if they won't listen? Remember what Mr. Spicer said? He could be sent back and tortured or killed. We have to try to save him, please, Alix. It's a matter of life and death."

Life and death. For a second Grandpa's voice whispers in my ear, telling me his story of the war. "It's good to be strong when you're needed," he'd say. Am I strong enough for this?

I can hardly bear to meet Samir's eyes. I look over at the man lying in a heap on the ground. We have to do something, and if we're not going to the hospital then we've got to take him somewhere a bit warmer at least.

Samir is tugging the man to his feet and they almost fall down again. I reach out and grab the man and before I can think anymore about it I've got one arm around our very illegal person and I'm helping him along the beach to God knows where.

If we're caught, we'll all be in deep trouble. Could I be deported for this? Where on earth would they send me?

As we stumble past the Lifeboat Station the mist has almost gone and there are now a few people on the main beach. I can see two dog walkers, at least one of whom I recognize, a jogger coming straight toward us and three weekend anglers down at the water's edge.

"Quickly, Alix. Where to?" asks Samir in a worried voice. I look around, feeling a bit panicky. Where do you hide on a Hayling beach? It's just wide open spaces as far as you can see, and it's miles to the rows of beach huts where we might be able to hide him, although they're usually locked. "Alix!" says Samir more urgently, shifting his grip under our man's drooping arm.

Then I remember the little hut on the Nature Reserve. There's a hole in the fence that me and Kim used to crawl through when we were in Junior School. We pretended we were Lara Croft acting out the games we played on Kim's computer. I loved Lara's cute khaki shorts and double gun holsters. I really wanted to be her when I was ten. Lara Croft could beat any enemy, overcome any obstacle. We used to practice kickboxing and ambush each other around the hut.

Lara Croft isn't scared of anything.

"This way," I call out, and start to tug everyone forward. Our man's so weak now I'm terrified he'll collapse on the beach in front of the dog walkers and the fishermen.

Pushing and pulling, constantly tripping over Trudy and her leash, we manage to get through the hole in the fence and past some very prickly bushes to the door of the hut. There's just one problem; a great big new padlock gleaming on the weather-beaten door.

8. Roll-ups

Everyone is looking at me. Samir has propped our man up against the door and is standing, staring blankly, hands hanging loosely by his sides. Trudy has her head cocked as if to say, "Sort it, Alix," and even the man has jerked open his good eye sufficiently to stare at me expectantly.

Sorry, I think, picking locks isn't on the National Curriculum! I don't come from a criminal family. We need a Bellows for that.

Then I realize that Samir isn't actually looking that worried. "There must be a way in, I'll check around the back," he says with a determined frown.

"Excellent," I say. "So when the police finally track us down, we'll be locked up for harboring an illegal immigrant and breaking and entering."

But it's only because I'm worried and frozen to an ice block. Maybe I should take Trudy and go home. But what would Samir do without me?

Just then our man is violently sick and starts to crumple to the ground. Samir manages to catch him and helps him to sit down.

I catch a whiff of the sick. That does it. I promptly throw

up on the grass. I warned you, I think furiously, I don't do sick. Trudy is getting too interested in the emptied contents of my stomach, and feeling weak and shaky I'm busy pulling her away from the stinking mound. So there's absolutely nothing I can do when Samir appears from the side of the hut carrying a sheet of transparent plastic.

"I took the window out. Quick, let's get inside." And he lugs the man off.

Glad to get away from my sick pile, I stumble around the hut and see that all I have to do is step onto a conveniently placed brick and wriggle through the gap. I climb up, pushing Trudy ahead of me, and suddenly we're all sprawled on the floorboards of a damp, empty hut. No lights, no furniture, nothing.

Trudy starts to nose about the hut, smelling every corner. The man rolls over and wraps his arms around his body, his eyes drooping with exhaustion.

Samir seems to be absorbed in making some kind of list. "We need blankets, dry clothes, food, candles..."

He's ticking off on his fingers just like Mum does with her online shopping. I've never seen him so worked up and excited. He's usually Mr. Ice Man around school.

"...maybe one of those little camping stoves, I think Naazim has one..."

"Naazim? Are you going to tell him?" My voice echoes strangely in the little hut.

Samir stops, his right hand suspended above his left, mouth opens and he's staring straight at me, eyes wary, like a fox caught in the headlights on a dark Island lane.

It's gone very quiet in the hut. Trudy has snuggled up against our man—what did Samir call him? Mohammed? I can hear one of the dog walkers on the beach call out, but the sound is too faint to make out the name of the dog. If it's Mrs. Saddler with Jeremy we're sunk. She can smell a rat miles away.

And then Samir takes a small plastic bag with a pack of cigarette papers and some stuff in it out of his pocket. What's he up to now?

Is he going to roll a joint, I think, going all tense. I'm already Miss Uncool of the Year for worrying about sheltering an illegal person, an asylum seeker who's been tortured and is probably dying of a brain hemorrhage. But drugs! I begin to plan what I'll say when Samir offers me a drag.

I'm asthmatic and I've forgotten my inhaler. I'm allergic to cigarette wraps.

What would Lara Croft do right now? She wouldn't give up and go home, whining about cigarette papers. Lara Croft would make a plan to save our man. She'd probably whistle up an elephant and ride us all out of here to some safe, cozy tomb in the mountains. Lara Croft makes things happen.

But Samir has made two roll-ups and lit them both, and even I know the smell of ordinary cigarettes. He offers me one and I take it. I've never smoked before and all I can think is, What would Mum say? which makes me feel about six years old. I suck cautiously on the end of the roll-up and actually it doesn't taste too bad. It's quite warming in the drafty hut.

Samir sits, smoking like he was born to it. That's why he can't run as fast as me, he's already ruined his lungs. He's picking stray bits of tobacco off his lips and I can't help noticing what a comforting color his skin is in the dim light. Not brown and not white, a sort of creamy shadowy color. I get this sudden urge to touch his hand. Does he feel as soft as he looks?

"So who are you going to tell?" I ask cautiously.

"No one," says Samir, and he's staring at me hard. "Not yet."

I look down wondering, If not now, then when?

"First of all Mohammed needs to get warm and dry," says Samir, and you can see he's still working it all out. "We need to get him some food." He's looking at me hopefully.

Questions start to thunder through my head. What will Mum say? Do I care? She and Dad are off in their own private worlds and I just seem to be here to clean the toilet and do the washing up.

"How long do you think we can hide him for?" I say. It'll only be a couple of nights at the most before the whole island knows, I think.

"As long as we can. Until he is better," says Samir. "We'll have to find someone to help him."

"Like who?"

"There are people who help asylum seekers. I need to find them on the Internet. They help people who couldn't get into the country legally," says Samir, and he's speaking in a more rapid, urgent voice. "You know, like Mr. Spicer said, some people who come in illegally are genuine asylum seekers but they couldn't convince the authorities. Mohammed is one of those, Alix."

He gives me such a desperate look and his eyes are wide with fear and worry. I stare back at him and I must have looked the same because suddenly Samir's face breaks into that smile which changes him completely. The line of his mustache darkens on his upper lip and the fear disappears from his eyes. "Anyhow," he says. "Won't it be good to have a secret from the adults?"

Well, that presses the right button. Not that I tell Mum much these days anyhow.

Mum! Oh my God! "What time is it?" I yell out, and practically squash Trudy as I leap to my feet. "I've been gone ages. Mum'll go ballistic!"

I throw myself up to the window and Samir calls out, "Don't tell, Alix, promise?" He grabs my ankles and his hands feel warm through my wet socks.

"It's okay, don't worry," I call out. "I'll be back as soon as I can. I'll bring some food and dry clothes."

Then I'm gone, running with Trudy out of the Reserve, past the Lifeboat Station, zigzagging past Mrs. Saddler and Jeremy before they can stop us, and I know it's insane, but in my head I'm kickboxing and somersaulting over obstacles all the way home. Just like Lara Croft. This is the most exciting thing that's happened to me since forever. I can't wait to tell Kim! There's no way we're going to let our man die or be deported, not after having heroically pulled him out of a churning sea, which was probably too dangerous for Lara Croft, even on an elephant.

But when I get home everything goes out of my head. As Trudy and I run into the house we hear a moaning and there's Mum, lying on the kitchen floor, rolling in agony.

9. Real Life

"Alexandra! Where have you been? I slipped over when I tried to get the butter out of the fridge." The white plaster on Mum's broken leg has a skid mark on it and her face is smudged with tears.

"You should have waited for me," I cry out, kneeling down beside her. There's a big blob of butter on the floor and it smells horrible. I'm nearly in tears too and Trudy's whining and trying to lick Mum's face, which is as white as sea mist.

"You were so long. Where were you?"

Her hand is sort of flailing around trying to grab my arm and for some reason it freaks me out. I feel suffocated and guilty and angry all at the same time. What am I doing trying to look after some washed-up stranger when my own mum's alone and in pain?

I'm just deciding I'll never leave the house again when her hand clutches the leg of my jeans. "Alexandra Miller!" she screeches, and she's off like a robot screeching in a monotone. "You've been in the sea, haven't you? What on earth were you thinking of in this weather? Can't you see how dreadful it would be for me if you went and got pneumonia right now? Your hands are like ice. Who would look after us if you were in bed, or in hospital or worse!"

There's that word again. Worse.

Mum stops to suck in air and I think one word. Dad. Dad should be looking after us, shouldn't he? Only I don't think it. I say it. Out loud. Mum just lies there, her mouth opening and closing like a fish, as if she can't think of anything worse.

I shriek at her out loud and in full Technicolor, "Why don't you look for him? Instead of lying around here all day. You could look on the Internet, or phone someone! Because he's somewhere, isn't he? Not nowhere? Then he can at least give us some money because I only get twelve pounds fifty a week for my paper route. You expect me to do everything. You're the adult. I'm the kid!"

And then the doorbell goes.

We stare at each other in horror and Trudy lopes down the corridor and starts pawing at the front door. I can see quite a large shape looming through the frosted glass.

Mum says quietly, "Open the door."

I get to my feet and scuff down the corridor feeling as though my body weighs a ton.

It's Bert from opposite. "I was just passing, Alix, and thought I'd look in on your mum."

He's got a big stalk of Brussels sprouts hanging in his hand and for once it's a relief to see him. "Thought she'd like some nice sprouts," and he hands me the stalk as he squeezes his beer belly past me into our narrow hallway. He's got his gardening boots on and he trails mud all over the floor.

He's sweating in his crumpled jacket, but he goes straight to the kitchen and heaves Mum to her feet and practically carries her back to her chair in the living room.

"Don't worry, Sheila, we'll call the doctor," and he nods to me but I'm already dialing.

I make everyone tea and then mutter that I'm going upstairs

to change. Bert can chat with Mum while they wait for the doctor. I run upstairs and close my door. I never want to speak to her again. Then I realize that actually she'll never want to speak to *me* again after what I said about Dad.

I didn't even know I thought all that stuff.

By the time the doorbell rings again I've got dry clothes on and I'm planning what I need to take back to the hut. I promised Samir and I can't just leave our man to die of cold, even if I feel bad about leaving Mum for a bit.

I go downstairs and it's the doctor. He's a tall, black guy, much younger than Mum. He's wearing a sweater and jeans, and he looks pretty casual, but he's carrying the right sort of bag and he takes charge straightaway. Bert looks relieved as he smooths down what's left of his graying hair. He digs deep into a torn pocket for his keys and says, "I'll leave you to it then," and I let him out.

When I go back in the doctor is flicking open his bag and Mum is asking him where he comes from.

"Nigeria," he says. "I'm doing some research here and paying my way with temp work."

Then I realize what the doctor could be useful for. "Did you bang your head when you fell, Mum?" I ask.

"Perhaps a bit," says Mum, looking rather vague.

The doctor feels her pulse and nods. He's got quite a nice sort of understanding face. "Did you lose consciousness, Mrs. Miller?"

"No."

"Have you been sick?"

"No," says Mum. But I have, I think, and so has our wounded man.

"Is that a bad sign?" I ask anxiously.

The doctor smiles reassuringly, his dark, smooth skin shining in the electric light. "Your mum isn't showing any signs of a head injury, but if she starts to be sick or gets very sleepy in the next 24 to 48 hours, then you should take her to the hospital. She might have a concussion."

And so might our man. How on earth am I going to get an illegal immigrant to the hospital five miles up the Island without anyone like Bert, Mrs. Saddler or even flipping Jeremy noticing? I almost break out in a sweat at the thought.

But the doctor is still going on, "...so your leg is fine, Mrs. Miller, but no more skating on the kitchen floor." Mum gives a little giggle.

The doctor leaves and it's sort of broken the ice between me and Mum. I scramble up some eggs and we sit watching an Australian soap together. I hate soaps, they pretend to be like real life, but they're nothing like it. Well, not like my real life, anyhow. But at least Mum and me are speaking again.

"How is your English course work going?" asks Mum.

"Okay," I say.

There's lots of other stuff I want to say, like, If we're not going to talk about Dad ever again, why can't we at least talk about Grandpa? Doesn't she miss him? He was her dad, after all, and he never let her down. But I manage to keep quiet.

"Are you seeing Kim tonight?"

"Dunno," I say.

"You can if you want, I'll be all right," says Mum, peering at me over the rim of her Best Mum on the Planet mug I got her last Mother's Day.

I'm just about to say I have more important things to do when my cell phone beeps. It's a text from Kim. *Hey party dude...* but before I can read the rest my phone rings.

"What time are you getting to mine?"

"What?" I ask. I haven't a clue what she's on about; it's been a really busy day.

"Spring Rave. School. Zak might be there. Durrh."

Zak's the 12th-Year boy I kissed at New Year at Kim's big sister's club. Right now he's the last thing on my mind.

I leave Mum and shut the door behind me. "You wouldn't believe what happened today…" I start, and then I stop. Suddenly I'm not sure what Kim would think. I'm not sure what anyone I know would say about this.

"You've been surfing with Al Qaeda around the yacht club," she laughs.

Well, then, I was right not to tell her, wasn't I?

1ᑌ. Supplies

It's already three o'clock and I have to catch the seven o'clock bus from Sandy Point to meet Kim at seven thirty. I haven't even washed my hair yet. Trudy starts to scamper up and down the corridor, skidding to a halt each time at the front door and looking up at me expectantly, her tongue lolling, ears flopping back. I can't help laughing; she looks so sweet and funny. I bend down to kiss her on my special white bit of fur over her nose. "We have a secret, Trudy. Shall we tell Kim?"

I so badly want to. We've been best friends since nursery and we do everything together. Kim stuck by me when Dad disappeared and Grandpa died and I lost my place on the basketball team because I went insane and screamed at the PE teacher. And Kevin, Kim's dad, came over when the drains blocked up and the toilet overflowed the week after Grandpa died and Kevin wouldn't take any money from Mum. "That's what neighbors do, Sheila," he'd said, and we live miles away from them. Kevin even brought her a CD of her fave punk band, The Clash, when she was in the hospital and I had to stay over with Kim.

But Kim has said some weird things this week about Samir and she didn't seem to notice what was happening in class yesterday, all the horrible comments and Lindy saying that even two percent of refugees getting to our country was too many. But look what's happened since then. Even I'm not sure if I should be helping Samir to hide someone from the police. If I tell Kim, what will she do? These days she always seems to be somewhere else inside her head, usually with Wolfgang Amadeus Mozart. She showed me his picture once. He isn't even that gorgeous.

Samir said I shouldn't tell anyone and I don't want to make things worse, do I?

I race upstairs and start grabbing some of Grandpa's old clothes. I pull out his dear, holey, blue sailing sweater. It still has a faint smell of his pipe, which I absolutely loved but Mum couldn't stand. She wouldn't ever let him smoke in the cottage, even when it snowed. I can't help wondering what he would say about hiding our man from the police. There's no time to think about that now.

I pull out two thick sweaters, warm trousers, a woolly hat, two shirts and some thick socks. I also find an old pair of boots Grandpa used to wear on the boat.

I push everything into a sleeping bag I keep for Kim when she sleeps over and then haul it downstairs.

In the kitchen I boil the kettle twice, first filling a hot water bottle and then a flask with coffee. Somehow we have to get our man warm and we can't exactly build a fire in the hut.

Trudy's beginning to whimper as I stuff bread, cheese, a packet of sliced ham, apples and a six-pack of chocolate bars into my school backpack. Then Mum calls out and I freeze.

"Alexandra?" Her voice is all wobbly and weak.

I dump the food by the front door, glaring at Trudy, who just ignores me and gives a little "whuff." I know she's building up to one of her excited barking fits as she senses we're going out. "Coming, Mum," I say.

If Trudy makes too much noise Mum will come stomping out on her crutches and see all the stuff.

I go into the living room. "I think Trudy needs another walk," I say.

"It's getting late," grumbles Mum, and then as Trudy lets out one short sharp bark, she relents. "All right, but make sure you're home by five, before it starts to get dark."

I look at the digital display on the video: 16:04. Talk about pushing it. "No worries," I call out cheerfully, realizing I sound like the surfers on her Aussie soaps.

Before she can say anything else I'm out in the corridor heaving on my backpack. It's going to be really awkward running like this, with the bulging sleeping bag in my arms. A bit like the waiter who runs the London Marathon with a drinks tray. I can't put Trudy on the leash but I'm pretty sure she'll just follow me.

As I sprint down the road and past the Lifeboat Station onto the main stretch of beach, the wind is reaching storm level and black clouds are piling up over the Solent. The sea is rolling up and down enough to make anyone feel sick. There's a really bad night brewing and I have to fight my way against the rising gale up to the hole in the fence. My arms are aching fit to drop off and the pack's dragging painfully on my neck. I just about get to the hut before I totally collapse and bang on the wall.

Samir's frightened voice calls out, "Who's that?"

11. Part of the Story

I'm probably just in time. Our man's shivering uncontrolla-bly. We pull all the clothes onto him and zip him into the sleep-ing bag with the hot-water bottle tucked in under the sweaters. He looks like one of those ancient Egyptian mummies by the time we're finished and all you can see is his face with its strag-gly beard and all those bruises and his lips blue with cold.

"I should have brought two hot-water bottles," I mutter, unscrewing the flask.

Samir puts his arm around the man's head and sits him up and tries to tip coffee into his mouth. Eventually he starts to sip and then takes great gulps. He finishes the entire flask in min-utes and then he seems to come alive a bit more and opens his good eye.

I can hardly bear to look at the other one, it's so bruised and swollen and it's stayed tight shut. What if it's gone blind or the eyeball's dropped out? I don't know anything about first aid and I'm pretty sure Samir doesn't either.

"Don't you think we should at least try and get him to a doctor?" I say, thinking about Mum lying on the floor.

"No!" Samir snaps back. "We don't know who we can trust." He's taken back his denim jacket from our man and put it on. Samir looks very cold too.

I think of the Nigerian doctor who seemed nice enough. But what if the first thing he did was call the police? Samir would never forgive me and that gives me such a strange empty feeling that I keep quiet.

Our man has pulled his hand out from the sleeping bag and started on the bread and cheese, stuffing great wads into his mouth.

"He's starving," I say.

Samir nods. "The smugglers didn't give him anything."

"Drug smugglers?"

Samir shakes his head. "People smugglers. They charged him $50,000 to bring him to England. Scumbags." And he glares around the hut as if he's looking for someone to thump.

"That's ridiculous, it can't cost that much," I say, and Samir gives me a pitiful look. So I decide to change the subject. "Did he have a job in...er, wherever he comes from?" I say.

"Basra," says Samir in a closed sort of voice. "It's in southern Iraq."

I nod casually but it isn't much help. I have trouble working out the bit of France I'm going to on French exchange next term. Geography's not my strongest subject. "What did he do there? Builder, plumber?" I've read in the papers that's what most foreigners do.

Samir gives a snort. "He was at university. He was studying engineering."

"Oh," I say. Engineering? Well, how was I to know? He doesn't exactly look like a techie type.

With all that hair tangled around his head and his scruffy beard, he looks more like one of the beggars from around the mall in Portsmouth. But I look again at his hands as he eats and they don't look like a builder's hands, they are too small, with thin, short fingers.

But then I see that Samir has closed down again, head leaning against the wall of the hut, his eyes staring blankly into space. Would he rather I left now? Maybe this man wants me to go as well. I caught his one good eye staring at me for a second as he munched on the bread and it wasn't a very friendly look. I don't blame him really. He's in pain, hidden away in a foreign country by a couple of kids. How does he know he can trust me? At least Samir speaks his language.

They probably think I just don't understand the situation, and let's face it, I don't really. I'm just the one who got caught up in this big, fat secret.

But it's a bit Lara Croft, all this. The kind of thing you see on telly and imagine happening to you, like an airplane crash on a desert island. I'd be the one who could run the fastest and find water first or keep the signal fire alight on the mountain and get us rescued. It's exciting and dangerous and our man needs our help and Samir needs me. So I'm not backing out now, am I?

It's getting darker and darker but I've forgotten my watch. "I have to go soon," I say, standing up. "What about your mum and dad? You haven't been home all day. Won't they notice?"

Samir doesn't speak and all I can hear is the howling of the wind in the pine trees around the hut.

Then he says, "My parents are dead."

It's so awful.

I just stand there. I don't know which way to look. When I look at Samir again his face is pinched and closed and I'm terrified he's going to start crying.

What do you say to someone with dead parents? Grandpa dying was bad enough, and Dad has managed to disappear totally off the face of the earth. But it's not the same, is it?

I look over at our man and his face is creased with pain as he wriggles about in his sleeping bag. What are *his* parents thinking right now?

I can't help wondering how Samir's mum and dad died, as if it was important and it completely isn't. I can't ask that in a million years. There's so much hidden in this little hut, and whatever I've dived into here, it's only going to get more complicated.

This man, Mohammed, is here without permission, he's an illegal immigrant, and Samir speaks the same language. Does that mean he's here without permission too? Does school know? Oh God, should I tell someone?

Samir startles me by speaking again. "I was sent out of Baghdad when I was nine."

"What do you mean, sent?" I ask.

But Samir doesn't seem to hear me; he just carries on in a sort of monotone, like a robot. Maybe he's had to tell the story a million times since he came to England and he's just totally bored with it.

"My father was a lieutenant in the traffic police. He wasn't a criminal. But one day Saddam Hussein's men took him away and put him in prison. We couldn't even visit him. Then they came for my mother. Naazim was put in the army. He was only fifteen."

"So what had your parents done wrong?"

"Nothing. They did nothing, Naazim says someone in the police had a grudge against my father and so they betrayed him."

"That's horrible," I say. "Didn't anyone stand up for him? I mean, it's so unfair."

Samir gives me a pitying look and our man shifts in the sleeping bag. Samir leans over and murmurs something to him and the man nods but his head is beginning to droop again. No one stood up for Mohammed either, it seems. Except us.

I sit down again and pull Trudy onto my legs for comfort, running my hands through her fur. What would I do if Trudy wasn't here anymore? Dad's gone, Grandpa's gone, Mum's useless. My dear little dog sometimes seems to be the only one left in the world I can depend on. How must it feel for Mohammed? He has no one.

Samir starts to speak again in that low monotone and I can barely hear him above the wind. "After they arrested Dad they came for Mum. No one told me anything. Then two days later the soldiers came and dragged Naazim away.

"He screamed at me that our father was dead. But I didn't believe him. I was so stupid."

I clutch Trudy more tightly, feeling scared and confused all at the same time. "But I don't get it, why are you here in England?"

"Uncle Sayeed woke me up in the middle of the night. He said they were coming for me." Samir looks at me and his eyes are wide with fear again. "They were going to put me in prison too."

I let out a gasp and clutch Trudy until she yelps.

"I didn't even have time to pack," Samir goes on. "Uncle Sayeed drove me to the airport and handed me over to a lady I didn't know. He gave me a kiss and told me to be very good and then I was taken onto the plane. The strange lady didn't speak to me at all and I slept most of the way. When we got to Heathrow Airport she disappeared."

"How old did you say you were?" And I'm wondering if all this was last year.

"Nine."

"So that was..." I make a quick calculation, "2002. Five years ago. You've been here five years?" I can't imagine leaving Hayling Island for six months. How can he stand it?

Samir nodded. "I came to England one year before the war and the end of Saddam Hussein. It came too late for my family."

"So what happened to you at Heathrow Airport?"

"It was terrible. I was standing there in my socks—I couldn't find my shoes because we left so quickly—and I felt so silly. I didn't know who to ask for help. Anyway, I didn't speak any English."

"But you speak it so well." Much better than Naazim, I can't help thinking.

"I had to, didn't I? Anyway, some social workers came and they put me into a children's home. There were kids there from Afghanistan and Somalia, kids who had arrived in England all alone, like me. We couldn't even speak to each other."

A children's home! Pictures of orphanages and Oliver Twist spring into my mind. "It must have been awful."

Samir nods. "I was so homesick and really scared all the time. The other kids were crying and fighting and the food was horrible. But then they sent me away from London to a foster mother who lived near our school."

"Was she nice?" I ask hopefully.

"She was okay," he says. "She wasn't my mother, though. And she smoked a lot..."

"What, in the house?"

"Yeah..."

"Gross."

"I thought my parents would get out of prison really quickly and fly over to England and come and rescue me," Samir says. "Then we'd go back and live in our house in Baghdad and of course Naazim would be there too. I just had to be patient and study really hard at school because English is useful in Iraq. I didn't understand anything, I was so stupid."

"You were only nine," I say.

Samir's head drops and he slumps back against the wall. Mohammed is staring at Samir with his good eye and I can't help thinking how shifty he looks. How do we know what he's doing here, or if we can trust him? But I feel mean having these thoughts so I don't say anything out loud.

"Auntie Selma escaped about six months later," Samir goes on. "She hates it here. She cries all the time for Uncle Sayeed, her husband. They don't have any children. She finds English difficult so she hasn't really made any friends." He looks down at his cigarette and then back up at me. "It took Naazim longer to get here, almost a year."

"So how do you know your parents are dead?" I ask. "Maybe they're just in some prison."

Samir's chin sinks into his chest. "Uncle Sayeed wrote and said that my parents had died in prison. We're stuck here forever."

So it was Samir's parents who were tortured. Meeting Mohammed must be bringing it all back to him. I don't know what to say and that terrible chill runs down my spine again.

But it seems to me that we are a little bit the same. Samir has to do everything alone, like me. All he's got is Naazim, who's only nineteen, and his Auntie Selma, who hardly speaks any English.

But that's where it ends. Samir's been through such a horrible time and all that's happened to me is that I've been left looking after Mum. No one in my family has been arrested or tortured or killed in prison. What would I do? How does Samir even get out of bed in the morning? We sit quietly for ages and I'm thinking how Samir always keeps himself apart from everyone else at school. It's as though he needs to keep an invisible wall around himself, not let anyone get too close, because his story is so awful. Like an ice man.

I get this strong desire to put my arm around him, but I don't know if he would like it. So I just reach across Trudy's back and pat his hand a bit and I can feel him relax so that's okay.

Then he sort of shakes himself like Trudy does after a nap and says in a lighter voice, "What took you so long? Thought you'd changed your mind."

So I tell him about Mum and the fall and the doctor and it's a relief to get off the subject of dead parents.

"Has he been sick again?" I ask.

Samir shakes his head. "He's looking a bit better." Mohammed has pulled himself upright again and both his hands are out of the sleeping bag and he doesn't seem to be shivering anymore. His lips are still very blue but he's eating more bread and cheese.

I notice the ham lying on the floor and pick it up. I hold it out but he just shakes his head vigorously. I glance at Samir.

He's got a knowing grin on his face and then he says in a deeply sarcastic voice, "Don't you listen in Religious Studies?"

"No," I shrug. "Me and Kim text each other."

"Doesn't the teacher notice?"

"We put our phones on silent," I say.

That does it. Samir starts to laugh. It's unbelievable. I wouldn't have thought it possible. Maybe it's nerves or exhaustion or hypothermia, he's still wearing his wet jeans, but his laughing gets louder and louder until it almost blots out the storm raging around the hut. Mohammed looks at him all startled and scared and he's got his bread poised in front of his mouth as though he's forgotten to take a bite and then he starts to laugh too, a deep, throaty laugh.

That sets me off, even though I haven't a clue what's so funny. And Trudy gets overexcited and races up and down, playfully nipping my hand. It's the best laugh I've had since before the broken leg.

It takes ages for us to calm down. One of us stops and then someone else starts and everyone just cracks up again. But eventually Samir and I throw ourselves down on the floor and Trudy flops between us and Mohammed, still grinning, gobbles down the last bit of bread.

"So what's the problem with ham?" I ask breathlessly.

"We're Muslim, we don't eat pig meat," says Samir.

"Oh," I say, feeling really dumb and then I nod toward Mohammed, "not much sign of concussion now."

Samir stands up. "I have to get home before dark or my brother will ask questions."

Of course he will, I think.

Samir says something to Mohammed, who nods, his eyes already drooping again, and then he wriggles back down in the sleeping bag.

"Will he be all right?" I ask.

"It's a million times better than the smugglers' boat," says Samir. "Meet me in the morning?"

I hesitate and our eyes meet for a few seconds. Then I say, "Of course," and we go out into the driving rain and the full force of the gale. A bus is arriving as we get to the road and Samir shouts good-bye and runs off. When I get home the video display says 17:13 and Mum's dozing in front of the telly. That's a relief, I think. She can't give me the third degree about where I've been, and I've still got time to get ready for the school dance.

I go straight into the kitchen and cook me and Trudy a huge fry-up, and as the storm rages like a battle around the cottage my head's full of prison cells, escape routes in the night, a fishing boat tossing on the Channel and a huge bag bursting with American dollars.

12. Listening In

I'm at the Rave, which is just another boring school party in the main hall. All I want to do is go home again.

The storm is still raging and everyone arrives screaming with their hair wet and telling insane stories about flooded roads and lightning strikes on trees. The Jayne family come in, arm in arm, wearing the same outfit: denim shorts, black tights, glittery vests and shaggy knee-high boots. Jess Jayne takes one look at me in a T-shirt and jeans and sneers, "Come in fancy dress, did you?"

She always makes me feel so small. Cow!

I look around for Kim but she's already made a beeline for Steven Goddard who plays trumpet in the band. He's helping her with her audition for the Youth Orchestra next week. She's so wired up about it when he hands her a cola she nearly drops it.

Why's Kim hanging out with him tonight? I thought we were going to find our 12th Years. Steven's such a geek. He's got his shirt belted into his jeans and his hair's slicked down with gel and parted at the side. His uniform is always immaculate too and he brings his books to school in a briefcase. His mum picks him up sometimes and I see her leaning against her silver Toyota, cell phone to her ear.

I can't see Mrs. Goddard with safety pins in her jeans.

I go over and say hi, but they're too absorbed in Mozart to notice me.

Steven's saying to Kim, "Remember the change to allegro in the fifteenth bar, they'll be looking for that."

Kim groans. "It's the fingering," she says, and Steven nods sympathetically.

I drift off and pretend to be interested in drinking a can of lemonade. Kim doesn't even look up. My 12th Year hasn't appeared. I'm alone again as usual.

In the end I go into the bathroom, lock myself into a cubicle and check my cell phone for texts. Maybe Samir has borrowed a phone and is trying to get hold of me. I gave him my number in case of an emergency.

There's no sign of him at the Rave. Probably couldn't afford the ticket. I had trouble scraping together five pounds to get in and I'm not even enjoying myself. But there's nothing on my phone.

Then I hear a crowd of girls shoving through the door, chattering and laughing, and it makes me feel even more miserable and lonely and unpopular. What has happened between me and Kim? We don't seem to be close anymore. There hasn't been a minute to speak to her about everything that's happened with Samir and our man. Whenever I try to start a conversation with her she just says, "Yeah, in a minute, just got to finish this concerto."

It's hard to know who to trust if you don't know what they're thinking. Can I trust Kim with my secret? Am I doomed to get everyone wrong all the time?

I can hear Jess Jayne, the leader of the Jayne family, with

Sarah Jayne and Emily, going on and on about boys and it's so boring.

I flush the toilet and just as it stops I hear Jess say, "Well who cares, everyone calls that muppet Two Percent now."

There's a general laugh and then a small voice says, "Alix doesn't." It's Kim! And she's standing up for me against the combined meanness of the entire Jayne family.

I open the door and everyone turns to look. There's a couple of girls leaning on the sinks at the far end and they're waiting to see what the Jayne family will do next.

Jess Jayne gives a snort and says, "Lindy's right. You must be desperate to stick up for him."

"Since when did you care what Lindy Bellows thinks?" I say, and Kim gives me the thumbs up. But my heart's thumping away in my chest. Emily and Sarah lean over and whisper behind their hands and giggle.

"Lindy's okay," says Jess, and she's tapping on her iPhone. The Jayne family are all rich snobs. "She's almost as mean as us."

Sarah and Emily shriek behind their hands.

"She likes to keep her nails sharp," hisses Sarah, and she pretends to rake Emily's face.

I feel a shudder go through me and Kim starts tugging at my arm to go.

Jess gives a snort and says, "At least she's not a dwarf like your little mate," she says, nodding at Kim, who only comes up to her shoulders.

Everyone's staring at me and Kim is almost wrenching my arm off but I can't leave it at that, can I?

"Yeah, Lindy's really lovely," I say, "until she decides to

carve her name on your face with her nails. Still, it'll match your lip gloss, won't it?"

A ripple of laughter goes around and Jess's mouth drops open. Result!

Kim literally shoves me through the door and we race down the corridor and leap in the air doing a high five.

We're back, I think. Then she starts going on and on about how nice Steven is and doesn't he have lovely lips, perfect for playing the trumpet, as if I'd notice, and how he keeps offering to go over her audition with her and should she invite him home to practice or should they keep it professional and only meet in school, until I can't stand it anymore and I blurt out, "So what did you mean about Samir when you said, If you like that sort of thing?"

Kim stops and stares at me, probably because I'm practically shrieking in her face, and says, "What?"

Her eyes are sort of clouded with worry and confusion and I wonder if I've got this wrong. "Samir isn't a sort of thing; he's a boy in our form who gets bullied for being foreign. They call him a Paki and push him around. He doesn't need Lindy on his back as well and I always thought me and you were the same on stuff like that."

My voice sort of trails off and then Kim grabs my arm, really tight, and says in this strained voice, "Of course we are. We think the same about everything, how mean the Jayne family are *and* Lindy Bellows and how yuck tuna melt paninis are and how dumb parents are most of the time and you know we think exactly the same about bullying and racism. We're against it. That's final."

"So what did you mean?"

"I didn't mean anything," Kim says.

But I can't leave it at that. "So why did you ignore me in the playground?"

"When?" she says amazed.

"I was shooting baskets with Samir yesterday lunchtime after Lindy had called him Two Percent in front of everyone. He's always on his own at break times. But you walked along the edge of the playground with your head down and just ignored me." I sound like a hurt puppy whining away but I can't help it.

"I had a practice audition and I had to get the Mozart absolutely perfect or Mrs. Whitehead would scream at me. I wasn't ignoring you. And just so you know, I never listen to anything Lindy Bellows says, I am not racist, I would never be racist and I can't believe you would think that of me." And her eyes begin to fill with tears.

Oh God!

I stand there feeling like a bit of rubbish washed up on the beach and then I feel Kim's hand slipping into mine. She gives it a squeeze and says, "Sorted?"

She grins up at me and the red lights in her hair are gleaming under the strobes.

"Sorted," I say.

And I nearly tell her right there and then all about Mohammed but everyone is screaming and the DJ is winding the crowd up and Kim pulls me into the middle and suddenly we're all jumping up and down to the Arctic Monkeys and I can't think about anything except the music and the strobes.

13. No Need to Ask Twice

Sunday morning looks like it's been washed out and hung up to dry after the storm. The streets are littered with broken branches, twigs and pinecones. You can see where the sea broke over the breakwaters and washed down Oyster Road. I bike through puddles all the way to Chaz's shop to pick up the Sunday papers. The sky's an amazing blue, but it's absolutely freezing. I can't help worrying how Mohammed is after such a terrible night. But I have to do my paper route first.

Anyway Kim is coming over soon. What will she say when I tell her?

When I arrive at the shop Chaz is still sorting out the orders so I glance at the headlines. There's all the usual stuff about drugs and wars, but one of the cheaper papers has this huge headline:

STOP ASYLUM MADNESS

It gives me a jolt and I start reading, almost expecting to see mine and Samir's names printed all over the page, accusing us of hiding someone. I scan down the page.

Bogus immigrants are ripping us off!

"These asylum seekers get everything for free. I'm bringing my kids up on the poverty line and we don't get nothing," says Carol Jones of Southsea, Hants.

One in five flock here.

Well, that's rubbish for a start, Mr. Spicer showed us the figures, we only get 2.7 percent of all those millions of people who have to run away. And I've seen where Samir lives. It's tiny.

What are you supposed to do if your family are arrested and tortured? If Samir had stayed in Iraq when Saddam Hussein was in charge, he would have been murdered too.

I feel myself getting so angry at the headlines I have to run instead of walk my paper route, pulling the cart at breakneck speed to cool down. Quiet little Hayling where I've lived all my life with Mum and Dad and then Grandpa, going to school with Kim and playing on the beach, suddenly feels so strange, with hidden corners and people arriving in terrible trouble. How do I know what the Islanders would think about hiding Mohammed?

"Still in training, Alix?" It's Bert's divorced son, leaning over the garden gate waiting for his paper. He's almost as bald as his dad and he looks as if he's wearing the same scruffy jacket. I skid to a halt and, pulling his paper out of my cart, I can't help wondering if he does everything the same as his dad. That would be a bit lame, wouldn't it? At least his dad is still around.

The huge Sunday papers feel heavier than ever and I have to make sure I leave them on a dry spot on people's doorsteps, otherwise they ring Chaz up and complain like mad, and with things the way they are at home, I need this job more than ever.

I think about Grandpa and what he would say about those headlines in the paper. He definitely wouldn't agree. Grandpa believed in justice and standing up for what's right. He wouldn't have let Mohammed die on the beach. He would have rescued him and kept him safe until he could get help for him.

I know this for sure because when Grandpa was a teenager like me he went on a real-life war adventure to Dunkirk. The British army was stranded there; hundreds of thousands of men on the beaches being bombed to bits. So his dad and his uncle, Wilf, went with all the other little ships to bring the soldiers home.

"There was five boats went from Hayling," Grandpa told me. "They all got letters from the navy telling them to come to Ramsgate and bring food for three days." He showed me his dad's letter, addressed to JP Knight, Grandpa's father. Him and his brother, Wilf, were boatbuilders, working at the local yard. "The navy knew who to ask," said Grandpa.

His dad and Uncle Wilf needed Grandpa to go with them to help crew. Grandpa had been out in all weathers on the boats since he was little. They knew they could rely on him.

I suppose Grandpa could have said no, like when I didn't want to help Samir with Mohammed. He was only fourteen, like me, well, I'm nearly fifteen.

Of course his mum was against it, said he was too young to get killed at sea. But Grandpa wouldn't listen. "I didn't wait to be asked twice," he said. "Fourteen is the right age to be if you're needed, Alix, and you're strong enough."

It was May 27, 1940, when they sailed out of the Solent in their little boat, the *Saxonia*. "It were almost twenty-four hours to Ramsgate, even leaving with the tide," said Grandpa. "We didn't get there until dawn the next day."

They had to sign on with the navy for a week. They pretended Grandpa was seventeen and they even got paid. "Five shillings," said Grandpa with a grin. "That's about fifty pence today."

The *Saxonia* was one of the smallest boats, only thirty feet long. "So they towed us with some others," said Grandpa, "to save on fuel. A right proper sight we was, all them fishing boats and paddleboats and barges from up the Thames. There were even a ferry from Hayling, the *Southsea Belle*. All chugging across the Channel to Dunkirk."

They knew they were near France when they saw huge plumes of black smoke on the horizon. "I didn't really understand about going into a war," said Grandpa. "It were like an adventure for a boy like me."

But then they got within range of the batteries firing from the coast. There were huge explosions in the water all around their boat. "A pleasure steamer near us copped it, and sank immediately. Our boat nearly capsized in the wash," Grandpa said. "We heard after that forty people on board had been killed."

It must have been terrifying. And I'm scared now, Grandpa, I almost say out loud as I put Mrs. Saddler's newspaper carefully on her Welcome doormat. I'm scared she's going to open the door and ask me what I was doing on the beach yesterday and then going into the Nature Reserve, because you're not supposed to go through the fence. I can hear Jeremy yapping away so I scoot off quickly before she opens the door.

It feels weird sneaking about behind the neighbors' backs. At least Grandpa had his dad to tell him what to do as they steered the boat toward the beaches. My dad's so useless.

"When we got close to the shore," Grandpa said, "we could see it was literally crawling with men. And there were long lines of them standing in the water up to their waists waiting to get away. They'd been there all day, freezing cold, and they was being bombed and shot at all the time."

It made me shiver just to listen to him. I could never be so brave, could I?

"There was bodies floating in the water too. I'd never seen a dead man before," said Grandpa, and he'd suck on his pipe and stare at the living room wall.

"One man was so weak he couldn't get in the boat, so I jumped in the water to help push him in. I was in it up to my neck. By golly, it were cold!"

But not as cold as the sea around Hayling in winter.

They got twenty men on board and then Uncle Wilf and Grandpa literally had to shove two others back in the water because the boat was overloaded. "It were terrible to hear them crying out to us," said Grandpa.

Once they were full they had to sail off to one of the big destroyers waiting a mile out at sea. The water was teeming with all the little ships ferrying the men to safety. "We worked solid for two days, hardly stopping for a bite or a bit of shut-eye," said Grandpa. "A lot of the men had dogs with them. We ended up with a little golden-haired spaniel. The soldier with her died of wounds before we got him back to Dover."

Mum would shake her head and bang the iron down hard on Grandpa's shirt whenever we got to that part of the story, and I'd stroke Trudy's soft spaniel ears and wonder how she would have coped in the bombing.

"We called her Maisie," Grandpa would say with a smile. "She lived for eight years. Plucky little thing she were."

After two days ferrying to and fro, the gearbox on the *Saxonia* went and Grandpa, his dad and Uncle Wilf decided to call it a day.

They turned around and headed for home, Spitfires and German Stukas slugging it out over their heads. It must have been so scary and amazing too.

"Uncle Wilf reckoned we saved two hundred fifty-three men all told," said Grandpa.

Now as I finish my route and head back to the shop I think, It's my turn now. No need to be asked twice, like Grandpa said.

But I'm terrified and I'm only saving one poor bloke. Grandpa saved hundreds.

14. Illegals

When I go into the shop Chaz is dashing around sorting out the magazine shelves and talking on his cell phone at the same time. He clicks off and hands me a chocolate bar and a paper to take home. I'm so hungry I start on the chocolate bar straightaway. So it takes me a few seconds to realize what Chaz is saying.

"You see," he says, and he's stabbing with his finger at a headline about asylum seekers.

I nod, my mouth full of fruit and nuts. "That's why I moved to Hayling," and I assume he's just going on as usual about how marvelous it is to live down here. But then he says something which almost makes me choke.

"Too many foreigners in London. Better to live among your own, ain't it?"

I stare at him but he just steams on without stopping for breath. "All them blacks and Hindus and what have yer, with their loud music and their goat curry and the smell. Something shocking."

He gets his comb out and he's combing back his thin hair and he raises his eyes to the ceiling as if to say, Me and you, Alix, we're the same, and I'm just stunned.

I want to scream right back at him, You racist pig! I'm nothing like you! But I can't speak.

My knees go weak just thinking about what he said. So I mutter, "Bye," and race off on my bike.

I didn't know Chaz was like that!

But then I didn't know half the class thought Lindy's Two Percent was funny.

I didn't know that racist bullies pick on Samir in school before last week.

And look at the mess I got into with Kim because I assumed I knew what she was thinking about. Samir and I got it all wrong.

So how can you tell what anyone thinks about anything unless you go around asking them out loud?

Do I have to walk around for the rest of my life starting conversations with, "Do you hate asylum seekers? Because if you do we'd better stop right now." Perhaps I should begin with everyone I know, or I think I know, first of all. Like Mrs. Saddler and Bert opposite and his divorced son and then there's all the teachers in school and what about Kim's mum and dad and her big sister, Jaxie.

My head's beginning to ache with all these thoughts when I turn the corner into our road. Kim's dad's car is parked up outside our house. It's still quite early, just gone nine, but that means Kim's here. I slow down to a walk to give me time to think. I've already decided to bring Kim in on the secret. But I have to be careful to give nothing away to the adults.

Who can you trust anyway?

"Hey, Ali," Kim calls out as I unlock the front door and go into the living room. Mum's still in her dressing gown and Kim's dad, Kevin, has a plate of buttered toast on his lap.

We hug and I say, "Let's go upstairs and listen to some music."

But Mum cuts in. "Just a minute, Alexandra. I want you to have some breakfast after that cold paper route. How's Chaz?"

I don't know what to say but Mum doesn't notice, she just carries on, "Such a nice guy. Came all the way down from London to take over the newspaper store after Alf and Queenie sold up. Seems to like it here, I don't know if he sails, does he, Alexandra?"

I shake my head and sit down. So Chaz has fooled Mum and probably Kevin now and should I add Mum to my list of people to interrogate?

Terrific, now I sound like a torturer!

Kim pours me some tea and Kevin puts three slices of toast on a plate for me and I have to admit it feels really good to be fussed over for once. Then Mum picks up the paper I've brought home and says in this really loud voice, "Look at these headlines, Kevin."

Kevin takes the paper, and reads out, "Bogus immigrants. Should at least get their facts right."

I've stopped sipping my tea and my ears prick up.

"Aren't they bogus if they sneak in on the back of a truck?" I say. I take a bite of toast and try to look casual.

"Or parachute down?" says Kim with a smile. At least she's listening, but it's not funny, is it?

"Everyone's got the right to seek asylum," says Kevin. "They're calling all asylum seekers bogus, as though they're coming here just to live off the state."

"Aren't they?" I say with an innocent look. But inside I'm worrying that maybe Kevin and Mum do agree with all that stuff in the paper. Maybe they think Samir and his family should be sent back to Iraq. I have to be sure.

"It's complicated," says Kevin with a sigh, and I think he's just going to stop there. He sips his tea and then he says, "Take the Poles, they're economic migrants from the EU, so they can come here and work, right? But then there's refugees. They come because it's too dangerous to stay in their own countries, right, Sheila?"

Mum sort of nods but I can see she's not sure.

"Like Henri who works in our kitchen," goes on Kevin.

"From Cameroon," says Kim, and I look at her in surprise. I didn't know about Henri.

"Right, he had to run away because he said something against the government and they would have killed him."

"So he has permission to stay here?" I say.

"He does now, but it took years as an asylum seeker. The Home Office only sent him his documents last December. Now he has refugee status."

"I don't get it," I say, confused. "Is he a refugee or an asylum seeker?"

Kevin rubs a hand down his face. "That's the difficult bit. You ask for asylum at the border, they call you an asylum seeker. Then when they give you permission to stay, which can take years, they give you refugee status. There's loads more things as well but you'll have to look them up on the Internet. I can't remember it all."

Kim's sitting on the floor braiding Trudy's hair, not really listening.

Mum's pouring more tea. Why doesn't she say something? Maybe she doesn't care; maybe she's against people coming into the country. It's not exactly something we've ever talked about. Why should we?

But right now I have to know exactly what Mum and Kevin really think and I can't keep guessing. It feels like they have to pass some sort of test.

"What would you do if an asylum seeker turned up in your street, hungry and cold, with nowhere to go?" I say.

Mum looks at me in surprise. "Is this homework?"

"No," I mutter, "it's just, well, you see it on the news all the time."

"I don't know," says Mum, fussing with the teapot again. Does that mean she passes the test and cares about people who have to run away from their countries, or fails it and I have to move out and live like a hermit?

"I'd probably call the police, right, Sheila?" says Kevin with a short laugh.

Mum nods vaguely and my heart sinks.

I decide to give it one more try. "But what if you knew they'd be deported and tortured, or even killed back in their own countries, then what would you do?"

"How do you know all that?" says Mum, giving me a strange look.

"School," I say shortly, and then I add, "Mr. Spicer did it in class on Friday, didn't he, Kim?"

Kim shrugs and picks up a piece of toast.

I look at Kevin and he rubs his hand across his face again. Then he says, "Well, in that case, I'd bring them in, cook them a great big plate of steak and chips and then see what we could do for them. Everyone has a right to be safe, providing they're not just spongers, right, Sheila?"

I look across at Mum. It feels like the most important moment of my life so far. Will she fail me?

Mum is looking thoughtful and then she says slowly, "Yes, of course."

I almost shout out with relief. So it's not just me and I don't have to go off and find a cave to live in all alone for the rest of my life and then Kim and I jump up at exactly the same time and race upstairs.

Before we're even in my room Kim starts rattling on about Trumpet Steven again, as if we were still at the school party.

"...and you know what, Steven says that one more straight run-through and he thinks I'm ready, so I won't stay too long today because Steven is coming over and..."

But I push Kim into my room, slam the door and put on the radio at full blast. "Shut up and listen. I've got something to tell you."

"I knew it!" Kim laughs. "I just knew you had something planned. What are we doing? All-night barbecue on the beach?"

"As if," I snort.

And then I tell her all about Samir and Mohammed and her eyes just get wider and wider until I'm sure she's lost the ability to blink forever.

15. Doubts and Fears

When I finish there's an awful silence in the room as Kim just sits there staring at me. What's she thinking? What's she going to do?

It would only take a nanosecond for Kim to rush downstairs and spill the whole story. Would she? Could she? And then she starts up.

"Oh my God! Are you mad? Crazy? Completely off your trolley? They'll lock you up, lock up your mum, lock up... I don't know, everyone, Trudy!" And she grabs Trudy by the collar and starts to cuddle her so fiercely, Trudy whimpers and struggles free.

"Quiet," I hiss. I go to listen at the door. "They'll hear." But Kim's really working herself up now.

"Hiding an asylum seeker! Do you know what they do about that? I mean, I don't even know, but I can guess. Wait till your mum finds out about this, you'll be grounded until you're fifty!"

She stops and I pray she's run out of steam, but then she sucks in her breath as though even worse thoughts have occurred to her and like a roller coaster starts all over again. "What do you even know about this man? Does he have a gun?"

"No, Kim, he doesn't actually have anything." But she isn't listening.

"He could be a terrorist planning, I don't know, a suicide bombing or something!"

"On Hayling Island?"

"Why not, no one would expect it down here. I mean, does he have a passport? How do you know where he is really from? How do we even know he is who he says he is?" she says, finishing triumphantly.

Finally she's run out of steam, her eyes blinking now with the extreme effort of trying to impress on me the enormity of what I've fallen into.

"I know it's possible," I say in a sort of calm voice, although it keeps wobbling as I look into her frowning face. "But I believe Mohammed's story. You've got to trust me."

Kim's staring at me with her wide, unblinking eyes, so at least I know she's listening. I almost don't want to stop talking for fear of what she might say next. What if she thinks we should go to the police? So I carry on.

"No one knows Mohammed is here, we just need a little more time, a day or two, that's all I'm saying, so we can find someone to help him. Samir says there are all sorts of organizations. Samir's been here for years and he knows..."

"Samir says...Samir knows..." mimics Kim, and her tone is really angry. "What the hell does he know about anything? He's not even English."

"So?"

"So how does he know how the system works? What about his parents, can't they do anything?"

"They're dead."

"Dead?" and the frown begins to fade.

Kim's world is very different from mine, full of her big, fun-filled family, none of whom have ever died. Not like me with Grandpa dead hardly a year and Dad gone off with the Gremlin, and absolutely nothing like Samir.

"They were tortured and killed by Saddam Hussein when Samir was nine," I say quietly. "He was taken out of the country to England. He was in a horrible foster home for nearly a year. Then his brother and auntie came over so he lives with them now. Kim, it's not safe for Mohammed to go back home to Iraq, and if we turn him in, that's where he'll end up. You have to believe it."

I slump down on the bed. It feels as though I'm trying to carry an elephant up a mountain all by myself. Trudy climbs up onto my lap and tries to lick my face but I push her away. Then I look over at Kim and she's wiping a tear from the corner of her eye.

The thing about Kim is she worries about stuff a lot, like her audition and not being late for school and always crossing on the green man, but she is the kindest, most generous person I know. In fact, all her family are the same and I don't know how I could ever think that she wouldn't at least want to help. But I really don't know what I'd do if she walked away from this right now.

As she stands up, I'm terrified that's just what she's about to do.

I sit on the bed and watch her standing in the middle of the room and it's like I can see her brain thinking through her mass of hair. Two whole minutes pass by on the clock radio and I'm practically holding my breath. Then Kim slips a glittery band off her wrist, shakes her hair and pulls it back tightly in a pony-tail and slips the band on. My heart's in my mouth as she starts to speak.

"Well, won't hurt to meet your man, will it?" she says.

Yeeesss! I think, relief flooding through me.

"We have to take him some supplies," I say.

"Does Trudy come too?"

"Of course, she's chief refugee spotter!"

"Well, let's hope she doesn't spot any more," says Kim grimly, and I lead the way out of the bedroom.

Kevin's just leaving as we get downstairs and Mum's dozing off so Kim and I can gather everything we need without any interference. Heaving bags of food, extra blankets, flasks of coffee and a fresh hot-water bottle, we let ourselves out quietly and walk around to the hut, Trudy scampering ahead.

It's still very cold outside but the sky is bright. The tide's beginning to turn, revealing a really good stretch of sand for running over. I can see a group of teenagers, older than us, hanging around the pillbox, drinking beer and smoking. I'm worried they'll get curious if they see us crawling through the hole in the fence, but we manage to skip through while they're distracted by a passing speedboat.

When we reach the hut I put my finger up to silence Kim. She nods but I can't see her face behind the huge bag she's carrying. What's she really thinking? There's no time to ask. I don't want to startle Samir and get into an argument before we're safely inside. So I call softly through the window and Samir's face appears.

"Have you got any food?" he says immediately, and then he notices Kim. His face shuts down as if someone has pressed the remote control. He stands back as we climb in.

I feel like a traitor.

16. Only Way to Get Warm

Mohammed's sitting up in his sleeping bag, shivering, and when he sees Kim he starts to shake his head and mutter. The look on his face is almost menacing, his dark eyebrows knitted in an angry frown and his mouth jabbering away in Arabic. I can understand the tone at least and he's really not happy.

"Kim's my friend," I say, but he just carries on in a low, almost threatening tone. I look at Kim and she shakes her head warily.

"Tell him, Samir," I say.

But Samir's kneeling down looking through the stuff, his face hidden, and I'm beginning to wish me and Kim were a million miles away. All that stuff about terrorists and plots streams back into my mind.

Then Samir hands Mohammed the hot-water bottle and suddenly Mohammed says, "Zank you, Aleex."

For a moment I'm a bit stunned. His voice is quite soft and there's a smile on his face.

"He does know a bit of English," says Samir, guessing my thoughts as he bends down to unscrew the flask.

"Oh," I say, wondering how much Mohammed can understand when we speak. I look over at Kim. She has a little frown on her face that appears when she's really concentrating or just worried about something.

Mohammed reaches out for the coffee and he lets out a little yelp of pain. Samir helps him to change position but he's giving out low yelps of pain all the time. I feel quite scared and I can't help thinking, What if he dies? It would be all my fault for not getting a doctor. I'd have to explain to the police where the body came from and why we didn't call them on Saturday when we found him. Shouldn't he be in the hospital? I mean, what would they do, lock him up? Not in Britain, surely, they'd operate on him or something. There's a deep cut on his forehead, which I can see through his straggling hair, and it doesn't look very healthy.

Samir says something quietly to Mohammed—I really need to learn some Arabic, seems to me a lot more useful than French right now—and it sounds as though he's trying to reassure Mohammed. Kim is watching them very carefully. Maybe she's planning what she's going to say to the police.

But then she says in her clear, ringing voice, "The best way to get warm, my mum always says, is a hot bath."

In this decrepit hut? I begin to imagine how on earth we'd heat the water, let alone where we'd put it.

But Samir's wonderful smile is spreading over his face and he says, "Great idea, but how?"

"Well, I suppose the only way is to go to Alix's," murmurs Kim as though she's really only thinking aloud, and then I realize she's serious.

"You what?" I explode.

Trouble is once Kim gets an idea into her head, it's practically impossible to shake it off. She might be worried about guns and passports and stuff, but now she's decided Mohammed needs a hot bath, nothing's going to budge her.

"I'll keep Sheila busy and you run him a bath. She won't notice a thing."

I'm speechless and meanwhile Mohammed is saying something in English, "Outside?" he keeps asking, and Samir is nodding and then he says something in Arabic.

Kim rocks back on her heels with a little smile on her face, more relaxed now.

"And you thought he was a terrorist," I mutter to her.

"Whatever, right now he needs to get completely warm. It's the only way, Ali," and she's staring at me, with her eyes unblinking like she does when she sort of wants to mesmerize me.

Then she scrambles to her feet, dusting down her jeans, and says cheerily, "Shall we go?" and Samir starts pulling Mohammed up and then everyone's piling out of the window before I have a chance to say no.

"Hey, gang!" I yell once everyone's standing outside the hut, Mohammed blinking in the morning sunlight. "What are we going to say to my mum? He's a bit old to be in Year 10 in case no one's noticed."

Out here in the clear winter light I can see Mohammed properly for the first time. He's so much older than us, maybe thirty, maybe older, it's hard to tell because he's such a mess and he stoops as if his back hurts.

But I can see he's a bit taller than Samir, with the same dark hair and skin. Maybe that's what everyone in Iraq looks like. His head is slightly bent, so that I can't see into his eyes. Can you trust someone who won't make eye contact, even if one eye is shut tight? Terrorist or frightened refugee; how on earth am I supposed to know?

Then Mohammed says, "No trouble, I go police, okay?"

"No way!" I say, a bit surprised at myself I must admit. Samir looks relieved. I glance nervously at Kim and she nods a bit more cautiously but she's still up for it.

"It'll be okay but you've all got to be dead quiet. And no smoking." I glare around at everyone and Kim looks surprised, but Samir gives me a grin.

We walk off, Mohammed leaning on us. Please don't let Mrs. Saddler come by with Jeremy, I pray fervently. What would I say? She'd hardly believe I have an uncle who's the spitting image of Osama Bin Laden. Which makes me as bad as everyone else, doesn't it, and I get annoyed with myself for even having these thoughts. I'm just terrified someone will see us.

It takes us ages to get to the house, but Kim goes straight into the living room where Mum's watching her quiz program.

"Hi, Sheila, I know that one, Beethoven's Fifth," Kim calls out, and Mum's face lights up.

I stand in the doorway while Samir and Mohammed sneak upstairs. Somehow Kim has managed to turn up the sound on the remote control so Mum doesn't hear the eighth and eleventh steps, which crack like a gun when you tread on them.

"Alexandra," says Mum, eyes still on the TV, "why don't you make us all some nice bacon sandwiches?" She's enjoying all the attention from Kim.

"Good idea, er, just one thing, does bacon come from cows?" I say cautiously.

"Good grief, don't they teach you anything at school? Why on earth do you want to know that?" Mum laughs.

I mutter something about geography and farming next term and she says, "Bacon comes from pigs, always has and always will."

Right, I think as I retreat to the kitchen, cheese on toast for the boys, bacon sandwiches for the rest of us. At least I won't make that mistake again. It's not easy hiding an illegal immigrant, especially one with special dietary needs.

While I'm in the kitchen making the snacks, I can hear Samir and Mohammed lumbering around in the little bathroom overhead. Our cottage is so small and the ceilings are quite low. There's gurgling from all the pipes as the bath begins to fill up. I'm terrified Mum's going to suddenly decide to stomp into the kitchen on her crutches and get suspicious.

Once all the food's ready, I take in sandwiches and tea to Mum and Kim and gobble mine down really quickly. Then I mutter something about checking that the gas is off. Mum is glued to the telly and Kim gives me a thumbs-up so I nip out the door. Back in the kitchen I pile the food onto a tray with two steaming mugs of coffee laced with spoonfuls of sugar, and I sneak out past the living room. I manage to get upstairs with the tray and knock on the bathroom door. There's a pause and some whispering. Then the door opens a crack and Samir's face appears. He looks relieved when he sees me and opens the door wide, holding out his hands for the tray.

But I get such a shock I nearly drop it.

Mohammed's standing stripped to the waist, his back to me, shaving in the mirror. But my eyes are riveted to three great ragged stripes slashed deep across his back, yellow pus oozing from the ends and beneath them a big burn, blistered and going black. And I realize that's why he can't stand properly upright.

A great spear of fear and pain and anger stabs into me. I

must have made a sound because he stops shaving and glances over his shoulder. His good eye catches mine and then his head dips quickly away.

My eyes fill up with hot stinging tears and I thrust the tray into Samir's hands and rush into my bedroom, kicking shut the door. I'm scared and angry and confused all at the same time and those horrible wounds are dancing in front of my eyes.

Why isn't Grandpa here? I need him to explain all this to me. And where's Dad when I need him? I pick up my cell phone and start to call the police, but I stop after the second 9. I can't betray Mohammed, and Samir would look at me with those pleading eyes if the police turned up and I'd feel like such a louse.

I have to make the right decision and as usual there isn't any time.

17. Being Invisible

There's a tap on the door and I look up. It's Samir. "Can I come in?"

I turn my face away; it's so red and blotchy. "You okay?" His voice is very quiet.

I don't answer. I'm sitting on the bed and I just go on picking fluff off the duvet cover and flicking it onto the floor. Samir goes over to the window and stares out. How does he manage to stand so still? He's like one of those ice sculptures. Even his breathing is silent, as though he practices being invisible.

Then I say, "I didn't realize..." I stop. Those wounds, they're horrific. I've never seen anything like it. How could anyone do that to him? To anyone? They're just animals, they're sick. We can't leave him like that any longer.

"Look, Samir," I say, trying to sound reasonable, but my voice is really shaky. "We must take him to the hospital, can't you see? He needs to see a doctor very soon or he might..." *die,* I think.

Samir goes on looking out the window and I think he hasn't even heard me.

Then he turns and says, "Mohammed is terrified the police will catch him and send him back to Iraq."

His dark eyes are very sad and serious. "He's just so desperate and so are his parents. They used up all their savings getting him out of Iraq." Parents? That feels reassuring.

Samir has this way of flaring his nostrils when he talks, which makes him look sort of passionate and angry all at the same time. He comes over and sits on my bed and he's leaning toward me as if he's determined to make me understand. He smells slightly of tobacco and also the soap he uses and it's a nice combination.

"Mohammed can't believe what's happened to him. He keeps saying, 'I'm just an ordinary person.' "

"So how come he got into trouble? I mean, Saddam Hussein has gone and the British and American armies have been in Iraq for, well, ages now, haven't they?" At least I think they have. To be honest, I don't watch the news much.

"Just because Saddam has gone doesn't mean everything's safe in Iraq. It's been four years since he fell—2003. I was ten years old. We were living in England by then and we watched it all on the news. But nothing has gone right in Iraq since. The West got it all wrong after they got rid of him. They sent the Iraqi army home and they thought they could control the country themselves. But instead, militias took over, terrorist groups, kidnapping people and killing them. And they all want different things. So it was like another war on the streets. You must have heard about the bombs? Suicide bombs, roadside bombs, car bombs?"

I nod but I still don't get it. Samir's face darkens as he sees me look a bit less alert, so I crease my face into an intelligent frown and try to look as if I'm thinking.

"Auntie Selma wants to go home. But Uncle Sayeed writes all the time and tells us to stay in England, finish our education before we think of returning. He tells Auntie Selma to look after me and Naazim; they don't have any children of their own. Last week Uncle Sayeed went out for bread, and a bomb went off on the next street."

He looks at me and I try to imagine a bomb going off by the local shops but it's impossible.

"That's very scary," I mutter.

"Very," says Samir. "Saddam has gone and there's a new government and we thought…" his voice trails off and his shoulders slump.

You thought you'd go home, I think, which seems perfectly reasonable. I want to say, If it's not safe, surely it's better to stay here in England, but I can't bear another dark look from Samir. I'm going to watch the news every night from now on and try and fill in the gaps myself.

So I say, "What happened to Mohammed, to get those awful wounds?" My voice wobbles at the thought of Mohammed's wounded back.

"Mohammed and his brother helped the British army when they were in Basra. They were both university students," Samir says. "Thousands of Iraqis did the same because they wanted to bring peace more quickly to Iraq. The British couldn't have managed without them."

"What's the problem with that?"

Samir gives a little snort and shakes his head. "The militias accuse them of collaborating with the enemy, they call them traitors and spies and they hunt them down. If they catch them, well…"

Samir stops and he's fiddling with the edge of my duvet and I know that look now. He's retreating back into his ice man world, shutting off because something bad is going on inside him, and I don't know what to say. I reach out like I did in the hut and just sort of pat his hand and even Trudy seems to know something's wrong because she pushes up against his leg.

This seems to melt Samir a bit and he looks up at me and says, "What many people in Iraq want is to be left alone to sort out the country themselves. But other people say they are scared what will happen in the streets if the British and the Americans leave. Will the Iraqi army be strong enough to keep them safe and bring about peace? Can Iraq become a proper democracy so that everyone has the same rights? Me, Auntie Selma and Naazim sit every night and talk about it until we get sick of it. We are so far away and we don't see anyone from Iraq, ever. Sometimes I feel like I'm marooned on a desert island."

"So it's sort of good you met Mohammed?" I say cautiously. Samir doesn't answer.

I start to imagine Mohammed going to live with Samir and Naazim and Auntie Selma and telling them all about everything they've missed in the past few years while they've been living in England. I'm really beginning to cheer up thinking about how great this will be for Samir and what a bit of luck it is that we were the ones who found Mohammed, when Samir says in a very quiet voice, "Mohammed and his family managed to get through all the bad times and stay safe on the streets. But then one of the militias kidnapped his brother."

Samir stops speaking and the room goes very quiet as if we are sealed off from the rest of the world. I watch the red spot on my bedside clock pulse out the seconds until a whole minute has moved on.

Then Samir says, "They killed him."

God. I almost stop breathing. I daren't even meet Samir's eyes. He's staring at the floor and I'm feeling very scared and it feels as though there's an elephant thundering through my insides. How can just words do that to you?

Then he says quietly, "They beheaded him and wrote on his back, *This is the destiny of spies.*"

The room spins and I feel as though I'm going to faint. I rush over to the window and throw it open, gulping down the freezing air. I can hear the shrouds jingling in the morning breeze over at the yacht club, and the Brent geese that come here every winter from the Arctic are bobbing about on the sea, their white tails flashing up and down.

Everything out there is just the same as it always is. Only nothing's the same anymore.

I turn back into the room. My voice doesn't really want to work and when I speak it sounds like a frog croaking.

"They must have been terrified."

Samir is looking very hard at me. It feels as though the temperature just dropped indoors.

It's as if all those pictures from the telly just appeared in my bedroom and I stare and stare at Samir and he stares back and I don't know who's more terrified right now.

He drags a hand across his face as if he's really tired and then he says in a dead kind of voice, "After they killed his brother the militia came for Mohammed. He only helped the British army for a few months but they kidnapped and tortured him. Those wounds on his back?" I nod, feeling numb with all the horror of it. "They did that to him. They hung him upside down for three days. Then his family bribed them and they let him go."

"He should go to the police and tell them all this stuff," I say, because it really does seem that simple to me.

But Samir shakes his head angrily, "It doesn't work like that. Mohammed asked for asylum in Britain. But the embassy said you have to prove you worked for them for a year, so they rejected his application. Someone said they could get him to England secretly. His parents used up all their money paying the people-smugglers to get him away safely. Now his parents have no money and no sons to support them."

"That's so unfair! Of course he should be allowed to stay, he helped us, so we have to help him."

"You read the headlines. The British are terrified of being swamped by people like Mohammed and me."

That's ridiculous, I think, remembering Mr. Spicer's millions on the white board. So few of the world's refugees even get to Britain. Then Lindy's nasty voice rings in my ear, "Two percent too many."

I'm staring at Samir's sneakers, which have broken laces and a hole over the big toe on the left foot. He really does need a new pair. What do refugees do for money if no one will help them?

"It's just not fair," I repeat, and I sound like a little kid who's dropped her ice cream on the beach.

"In England," says Samir, "you think that everything has to be fair and if it isn't you go on the telly and make a huge fuss. It's not like that for us."

I don't trust myself to speak again.

Then he says, "Once there was a bombing three streets away and my uncle found a human finger in the garden. Life isn't fair."

Samir takes two cigarettes out of his pocket and offers me one.

"What about Mohammed?"

"He's in the bath, he's okay for a bit," says Samir.

I glance at the door to make sure it's properly shut. Kim's keeping Mum occupied so we should be okay. I feel myself relax and say, "Only if we lean out the window. If Mum smells smoke she'll go ballistic."

Samir smiles almost his entire special smile and lights my cigarette for me. We push open both windows and dare each other to lean out farther and farther until Samir is practically hanging on to the drainpipe.

"You'll fall!" I'm laughing so much I choke on the cigarette and then he waves his arms about as if he's swimming. The air is bitingly cold but the smell of sea and salt clears my head. I grab his jacket and pull him back in and then I throw the half-smoked cigarette onto the grass below.

"I'm in training," I say, "don't want to clog my lungs up with that stuff."

"My foster mother used to say, 'Smoking's good for you sure enough, Sammy, keeps the germs away,'" says Samir, grinning. I laugh at his attempt at an Irish accent.

"I believed her when I was little. But now I'm hooked." He smokes right down to the filter and then stubs the end on the outside wall.

"Chewing gum?" he's offering me a wrapped stick and we sit there for a while chewing, the minty taste refreshing my mouth.

"Do you think people can read minds?" Samir suddenly says, and I feel a chill flit down my spine. I thought we were over the weird stuff.

"Not sure."

"After my father was arrested," he says, "I was even too

scared to think sometimes in case Saddam Hussein could read my mind."

"Will you ever go back?"

Samir shrugs. "Naazim says life in Iraq will get better. He says one day the Iraqi government will bring peace, and life will be as safe there as it is here. But for now we must work hard and make something of ourselves. Then we can go home and help to rebuild our country. My parents wanted me to be a doctor..." and his voice breaks up.

I feel tears welling up and I don't want Samir to see, so I bury my head in Trudy's soft, warm fur.

He gives a little cough to clear his throat and says, "Naazim wants to be an architect."

Naazim, a student? That's hard to imagine. Nasty Naazim with his greasy overalls and broken English.

Samir guesses what I'm thinking and he says, "Naazim was top in all his classes in Baghdad. But he was forced into the army at fifteen when our father was arrested. He'll catch up one day. He's much cleverer than me."

My face goes red and I turn away. Trust me to get it wrong again. So I change the subject. "What do you think Mohammed wants?"

Samir gives me a worried look. "To be safe again. But his wounds feel worse every day. Do you think they're infected?"

I shrug, I haven't a clue. How much longer can we go on before we give in and call an ambulance? A foghorn sounds in the Solent and it makes me feel so lost and lonely sitting here in my bedroom with Mohammed's awful wounds between us, like some enormous beast waiting to pounce.

Then the door opens and Kim comes in. "Is it time to go back?" she says.

Samir stands up and I say, "You take Mohammed to the hut. Kim and me will go to the pharmacy and get something for his wounds."

"But you'll come straight back?" says Samir anxiously, and he's frowning toward Kim.

"Of course," I say.

18. Chips and Smugglers

The sun's shining as Kim and me pedal up the road, seagulls whining overhead in the clear air. A helicopter buzzes over the Solent and there's the roar of a motorboat setting out from the boatyard at the end of our road. I've given Kim my mountain bike and I'm on Mum's old shopping bike so I get out of breath quickly, what with trying to keep in a straight line and filling Kim in on Mohammed's story.

"What do you think would happen if the police found out?" says Kim.

"Dunno."

We have to go into single file as some cars come past. When we're back side by side I say, "If you read the papers it looks like everyone hates asylum seekers."

"We don't."

"No, but the trouble is we don't know who else thinks like us."

And that's the problem, I think. If me and Kim don't know who to trust then how on earth can Mohammed and Samir hope to feel safe?

We cycle along the front and then Kim calls out, "I'm starving, it's ages since we had that sandwich. Jaxie's working at the pub today, shall we go up there and get some chips?"

I hesitate. It's almost two o'clock and then I think, Mohammed won't die if we're another hour and it's so great being in the open air, hanging out with Kim after all the insane stuff of the last few days.

So I say, "Cool, let's go."

We pump our pedals north through the Island and onto the bridge across Langstone Harbor to the mainland. The sea stretching out either side of the bridge is a choppy gray color whipping into little white flurries, and I can see the water lapping right up to the seawall. The tide is still high and won't turn for another couple of hours. When we get to the pub people are already sitting in the sunshine on wooden benches, throwing crisps and pork scratchings to the ducks and a single swan bunching up on the water.

Jaxie comes out to collect glasses and seeing us calls out, "Hiya, how about some chips?"

She disappears and comes back carrying a tray with two enormous portions of chips, ketchup, salt and vinegar and two glasses of cola, with ice and a slice of lemon.

"Hope you remembered the vodka," says Kim cheekily, and Jaxie messes up her hair, which Kim hates.

"Thanks, Jaxie. We'll clear some glasses for you when we've finished," I say.

She gives me a big grin and says, "You're all right, Alix. How's your mum doing?"

"Okay," I mumble through a mouthful of chips, and Kim and I settle down to watch the yachts bobbing about on the swell.

A boy rows up and takes a packet of crisps and a couple of cans from a man on the quayside and I think how great it would be to sail around Britain, stopping in pubs for chips and never getting off your boat. I'd just started to learn how to sail with

Grandpa when he had his first stroke, and after that he couldn't take the boat out anymore.

The sun on the benches gets warmer and Kim stretches out, pulling her jacket around her, and dozes off. I collect up a great stack of plates and glasses and wander around the back of the pub to the kitchen door. Trevor, the cook, is taking a cigarette break in the little garden and no one else is around. Must all be busy serving, I decide.

The sink's piled with dirty stuff so I clear it, and squeezing loads of frothy dish soap, fill the sink and start to scrub the greasy plates. The pub's very old, with low ceilings and thick oak beams, and I imagine I'm a cabin boy in the galley of one of the old sailing ships, slaving away all day, adjusting my legs to the roll of the ship. Maybe I'd be part of the Langstone Gang.

"That's what your grandfather would have liked!" Mum used to joke.

Grandpa told terrific smuggler stories when I was little. "The Langstone Gang were notorious," he said once when we were having breakfast before school. "They brought in all the things the government wanted taxes for, such as spirits..."

"Why did the government want to tax ghosts?" I'd asked.

Grandpa laughed and finished buttering my toast. He often took me to school back then. We'd go in his old Nissan Sunny.

"Not those sort of spirits," he said. "Drink, you know, like whisky and brandy."

"Oh, that," I said, nodding casually. The adults drank brandy on birthdays sometimes.

"They smuggled in tobacco..."

"For your pipe?"

Grandpa nodded, "And lace, fine silks and wine."

"Didn't the police catch them?" It all seemed very exciting, sailing around Hayling Island with smuggled stuff in your boat. Did smuggled mean stolen?

"They didn't have police hundreds of years ago. Customs officers chased smugglers. But the Gang was too clever. They didn't keep their contraband on the boat; they towed it behind them, beneath the surface of the water. Then if the customs boat appeared they'd cut the towline and the cargo would sink to the bottom."

"So they lost it?! What's the point?" I giggled.

"Aha!" Grandpa would twinkle. "They knew exactly where they'd dropped their contraband and they would go back at low tide and find it. The customs fellas hadn't a clue."

"You'd know where to find the countryland again, wouldn't you, Grandpa?" I'd say. I always got the long words wrong when I was little.

"Wouldn't he just!" Mum laughed, and Grandpa would sit back in his chair, a knowing look on his face, sucking his empty pipe.

What would Grandpa think of people smugglers? I wondered, watching froth drip slowly down the side of the beer glasses. What would Grandpa say about those scumbags who pretend they are bringing terrified asylum seekers to a new and better life?

"Mohammed just wanted to die when he fell in the sea," Samir had told me. "He'd never been so cold in all his life. Iraq is really, really hot. I remember when I first came here; it felt like I was living in a giant air-conditioning unit, twenty-four seven."

"Wow, Alix, you're a real star!" Jaxie's shrill voice breaks into my dreams and I turn, towel in hand, drying the last of the glasses.

I shrug. "It's nothing."

"Clearing the lunchtime crockery, I wouldn't call that nothing, where's that lazy sister of mine?" Jaxie digs into the pocket of her jeans and pulls out a five-pound note. "Here, slave wages."

"Thanks, Jaxie!" I grin and go back outside.

Kim's sitting up, throwing the last of her chips to the swans. We jump back on our bikes and pedal furiously to the big pharmacist in the village.

The pharmacist is very helpful on infected wounds.

"But it sounds like you really need to get your uncle to a doctor. I'm sure he needs antibiotics," she says anxiously.

She's very thin and quite young-looking really, and even though she's wearing a white coat I think she could be just a student. I can see she bites her nails right to the edge.

"My uncle hates doctors," I say, and Kim nods. "So we'll just have to manage by ourselves."

We come away with a huge bag of antiseptic wipes, creams, dressings and miles of surgical tape.

"Do you know what to do with all this stuff?" I ask Kim. She shrugs. "Trial and error, I suppose."

We cycle back to my house, dump the bikes and collect Trudy, who's desperate for a walk. Then we go off to the beach. As we arrive outside the hut I get this strange feeling, as though something has changed.

I climb through the window, calling out warily, "We're back."

But Samir and Mohammed are both jammed up against the wall, their faces creased into worried frowns, and standing in the middle of the hut is Lindy!

Oh my God! Now we've had it!

19. Criminal Record

"What's she doing here?" I say in a voice hoarse with shock. Mohammed and Samir shrink even farther against the wall, and Kim bends down to hold Trudy's collar.

"You promised," breathes Samir in a voice brimming with accusation and hurt.

"What?" I say.

"You told, didn't you?" Samir says, flashing an angry look in Kim's direction.

I look to Kim.

"It wasn't me, Alix!" says Kim, and I know it wasn't.

I swivel around and square up to Lindy. Standing so close to her in that damp hut, I think about her heckling, "Two percent too many!" in class and how she unfurled her spear-nail in Samir's direction. If she lets loose with that thing now it'll have to be a Lara Croft moment, with me kicking her hand away while Samir lugs Mohammed out of the hut. Trouble is I haven't a clue which leg to use.

"What do you want?" I demand, trying to look hard. She's about my height and her pale face is covered in freckles, her frizzy red hair pulled back tight into a band. She's wearing a very short denim skirt, a white zip-jacket with a furry hood and floppy suede boots.

She gives me a look as if to say "oh puhleese" and says in a bored voice, "Just hanging out. It's a free country."

"Are you meeting Terrence on the beach?" asks Kim in her most worried voice. She's crouching on the floor beside Trudy looking like she wants to sink through the floorboards.

"Maybe," says Lindy, and I feel myself tense.

Kim and I exchange looks. She gives me a quick shake of the head, urging me not to wind Lindy up.

So I say in a slightly more friendly voice, trying to sound sort of casual, "How did you know we were here?" But inside I'm already flinching as I see her straighten her fingers out. "Saw you when I was waiting for Liam down at the pillbox."

"Liam from the carnival?" I ask, and Lindy nods but she's not looking quite so confident. Liam's about twenty, with shoulder-length greasy hair and acne scars all over his face. He absolutely never speaks.

"You're not going out with him!" snorts Kim contemptuously, before she can stop herself, and I see a hurt look flicker across Lindy's face.

Now who's doing the winding up? Thanks a lot, Kim. But then I have another thought. If Lindy feels sort of embarrassed, maybe she does have a human side. Let's hope so, because right now we don't need any more enemies.

"Who's he?" says Lindy, pointing the nail at Mohammed.

"My cousin," says Samir quickly.

"Yeah, right," says Lindy, and she gives a loud sniff. I feel myself getting all hot and angry. Kim lays a cool hand on my arm as if she can read my mind, and I stay under control. For now anyhow.

Then Lindy says, "So, what're you doing here?" She throws a contemptuous glance around the hut. How does she manage to make me feel so small? Just like Jess Jayne.

"They're just camping out," I say, and it sounds so lame.

Lindy reaches out one booted foot and pokes the end of Mohammed's sleeping bag. He shifts his legs gingerly.

"Hiding out, more like," says Lindy with a nasty laugh. I hear Samir suck his breath in sharply.

"On the run, is he?"

"Don't be ridiculous!" It's Kim, speaking in the voice her clarinet teacher uses when she moans she can't play something. Kim mimics her beautifully and even Lindy's face flickers for a second. "Like we said, just camping out."

Lindy doesn't say anything but she's looking all around the hut and then she spots the bags from the chemist.

"Has someone hurt themselves?"

"Don't say anything," warns Samir. "You can't trust her." But Lindy's already riffling through the bags, pulling out tape and dressings.

"Must be a big cut. Is it him?" She points to Mohammed's bruised face. "This stuff's useless for a black eye."

"What makes you such an expert?" asks Kim.

"St. John's Ambulance," says Lindy.

"You're kidding?!"

"No," says Lindy slowly, as if she's speaking to a complete retard. "I've been going for months. I'm going to be a paramedic."

"In your dreams." Kim laughs. "They're hardly going to take someone with a criminal record."

She means the shoplifting.

Lindy gives Kim a hard stare. I tense, ready to leap at Lindy if she swipes out with that claw, and then she says in a loud voice, "They chuck it out once you're eighteen."

The ringtone for Kim's cell goes off and everyone jumps, even Lindy.

Kim pulls her phone out of her pocket and says, "It's Mum."

I nod to her, and we all stay quiet. No point in making the adults suspicious.

She answers it. "Yes. No. With Alix. Do I have to? Okay. Yeah, yeah, I'll leave right now."

Kim puts her phone back in her pocket and says, "I have to go, Alix. Mum wants us all to go to the Home and see Gran. She's not very well again." She gives my arm a squeeze and I nod reluctantly.

On my own again, I think as I watch her wriggle out of the window, and how am I going to persuade Lindy to keep this secret?

"Don't tell Terrence anything, Lindy. Will you? We can trust you, right?" I give her a pleading look.

Lindy just examines her nails looking bored.

Samir mutters something to Mohammed in Arabic and then Mohammed unzips his sleeping bag and slowly gets to his feet. Even though he looks a bit less wild now that he's had a shave, Lindy looks surprised at facing a full-grown man. She takes a step back and trips. Mohammed reaches out and catches her arm.

"Aleex okay," he says in a low, weak voice. He's swaying on his feet slightly. "You help Aleex, okay?"

Lindy's pale face goes red and she snaps, "All right, keep your hair on," and brushes the hand off her arm. Smoothing down her skirt, she says, "Haven't seen Terrence for days anyway. Couldn't care less about him. Hope he's dead."

Samir and I exchange looks. We have no choice but to trust her, and maybe if she really knows first aid she can be useful right now.

Samir helps Mohammed to take off his, well, Grandpa's, sweater and show Lindy the wounds. Lindy doesn't even flinch, which makes me feel like a right wimp.

"Didn't you get scissors?" she says scornfully, rummaging about in the bags. "Who gave you this stuff? And no disposable gloves."

She's pulling out tubes and packets, heaving a big sigh as if we're just a bunch of idiots, which, let's face it, in relation to emergency treatment of war wounds, we are. Where on earth did she learn all this? I've never seen her so much as put her hand up in school. I thought she was totally dumb.

"You'll have to change it tomorrow," she says. "He's got pus. It's all infected." There's a dirty piece of gauze in her hand and she grabs a plastic bag. "Here," she snaps at me. "Hold this open."

I do what she says.

When she's finished and Mohammed is getting dressed again, she says, "He needs antibiotics."

"We know," I say, watching her carefully.

Mohammed murmurs something as he lowers himself with difficulty back into the sleeping bag.

Samir nods and says, "It's feeling better, Lindy. Thanks."

"I'm off then," says Lindy.

And the weird thing is she doesn't ask anything more about Mohammed. That feels almost as bad as asking loads of questions. I go outside the hut with her and say, in a quiet voice, "You've been brilliant. Remember, just our secret."

She hesitates for a second and I even think about offering her money.

But then she turns away and walks off through the bushes and trees, back toward the road.

Where is she going now?

2U. On the Beach

"I have to go," says Samir.

"Me too," I say, but I'm still worrying about Lindy. You just can't trust her, she's meaner than the Jayne family and she's a Bellows. Everyone steers clear of that family. The oldest brother is in prison. They're all thugs. For all we know she could go straight to Terrence and his gang and give us away.

Samir murmurs something to Mohammed who's already half asleep again. Then we climb out the window and start to push through the bushes around the hut and I'm thinking, it's actually not that difficult to spot from the beach. Lindy saw us coming this way, so who else might? Mrs. Saddler? Chaz?

"He can't stay here forever," I call over my shoulder to Samir.

"I know," says Samir. "I'm working on it."

"And we definitely can't trust Lindy," I say.

We crawl through the hole in the fence and walk around behind the Lifeboat Station as the Solent opens out in front of us.

It's very cold but clear and you can see the outline of West Wittering on the other side of the water just a mile or two away to the southeast. At low tide when the sand flats off East Head are uncovered you could almost swim there.

"It reminds me of the Tigris," says Samir, his hands shoved

in his pockets, the hood of his sweatshirt pulled over his spiky hair.

"There's a sea in Baghdad?" I ask.

Samir laughs. "The Tigris is a river; it goes right through the city. Iraq is the land of the two rivers, the Tigris and the Euphrates."

I have to admit I haven't really thought much about Samir's country before. "So what is there in Iraq other than rivers and bombs?" I ask, not really concentrating because I'm wondering if I could fit a run in before it gets dark. Me and Trudy could do with the exercise.

Samir's gone all quiet again and I look over at him staring out to sea. Is he wondering how long it would take to sail to Baghdad? I mean, you definitely can't swim there. Even my geography's not that pathetic.

"That seems to be all the people here know about Iraq. Bombs and killings. There's so much more..."

His voice fades away and I'm a bit stumped so I say, "Do they have fish and chips in Iraq?" and Samir grins.

"We used to have picnics by the river. My dad used to buy fish fresh from the fishermen. Then we'd cook it with mint and garlic on charcoal under the palm trees. Everyone does it, we call it *mazgouf.*"

"*Mazgouf.*" That felt good to say. I can almost smell the barbecue. And palm trees? "Do you get coconuts?"

"Not in Iraq," says Samir. "They're date palms. We have the best dates in the world and we make this syrup called *dibis.* It's sweet like honey. You dip your bread in it."

I've never seen a real palm tree but I always thought it would be cool to climb one barefoot like they do on telly.

"So your palm trees, do they bend over like the trees on

Hayling?" And I point to the scrubby trees on the edge of the Nature Reserve. The wind has pushed them so hard they look like they are going to tip over.

"They bend in the wind really low but they never fall down," says Samir. "My father used to say we Iraqis are like the palm trees. We'll never break, whatever happens to us. Our roots are too deep in the land."

"You must miss it a lot."

We're walking fast now to keep warm and Samir says, "What I miss is playing football after school with Daoud."

"Who?"

"Da-oud," he says again slowly. "It's like David. He was my best friend since we were born. We did everything together, always sat next to each other in class. I don't have a friend like that here."

He looks at me and our eyes lock for a few seconds. Then he looks away and I kick about in the sand wondering what to say. He must feel so lonely sometimes, his parents dead and everything he knew, friends, school, shops, all gone.

I look at the sea over the tall grasses waving about on the dunes and think about everything I love about my home, the beaches and the surfing waves and all the different birds, which are like old friends really. The air smells of salt and seaweed with a whiff of engine oil dumped by tankers crossing the Channel miles away.

My family have lived here forever. What if I never saw it all again?

Samir is rolling up a cigarette. He lights it, takes a drag and passes it to me. I take a small puff and pass it back.

"Naazim would go mad if he knew I smoked," he says. "Once Daoud had a cigarette," he says, and gives a little laugh.

"He stole it from his uncle. We were only six. We thought we were really tough lighting up. Took us almost a whole box of matches to even get started. But when we took a puff we couldn't stop coughing and then Daoud was sick all over his new shoes!"

I say jokingly, "Smoking can kill you..."

"Bombs can kill you," cuts in Samir.

Once again we fall silent. There's a lot of difficult stuff to avoid, I think, and then I decide that there is something I really need to know.

"If you're worried they'll deport Mohammed, why do you think your family are safe here?"

"No, it's not like that," says Samir, and he digs his hands in his pockets and looks away. Then he says, "We have proper permission to stay now. It's called refugee status. We're not asylum seekers anymore, we can work and I can go to school. That's what Mohammed needs." He sucks back the last of the roll-up and stubs out the end on a rock. "It's my job to find someone to help him."

"*Our* job," I remind him, and he gives a little nod. "And we have to do that before Lindy starts blabbing and Terrence kicks off."

We reach the road and as I watch Samir go off on the bus I can't help wondering who on earth can magic up a brand-new life for our asylum seeker.

21. Secrets and Lies

As I stroll home from my paper route the next morning I get a mega shock. In front of our house is a police car. Have they discovered the hut and found Mohammed? What's Mum going to say? I'm about to be arrested, maybe even deported.

"Had a burglary?" It's Mrs. Saddler, nosing around as usual. She's leaning over her garden gate, Jeremy sniffing at her heels. "Lot of comings and goings at your house lately," she goes on, eyeing me curiously.

I don't even dare to speak; my voice would give everything away.

My legs are practically collapsing as I go into the house. Two huge policemen are standing in the living room in stab vests, their radios crackling.

Mum's looking quite bright and cheerful with her bad leg up on the sofa.

"These two gentlemen are looking for smugglers. Your grandpa would have loved this," she says with a laugh.

"You must be Alix?" says the biggest policeman. He has a rough voice and seems to shoot his words out as if from the barrel of a gun.

I stare warily at him through half-closed eyes. What if he can read my mind and he already knows everything about

Mohammed and he's just waiting for me to give myself away? At least we don't do torture in this country. Or do we? Mohammed's ruined back swims in front of my eyes. I feel sick.

"We're going house-to-house. Want to know if you've seen anything suspicious on the beaches," the big policeman barks out.

I stare at him for a couple of seconds and then bend down to unclip Trudy's leash, playing for time. This is my chance to put things right, to tell the truth and then let them decide on the right thing to do.

But what is the right thing? If I give Mohammed away they could just shove him on a plane back to Iraq.

So I say in a bored voice, "Nothing ever happens down here, does it?"

That's it, then, I think with a shiver. I've lied to the police. I bury my face in Trudy's neck and wait for the handcuffs to descend.

"You must walk on the beach every day with your dog," says the other policeman. His voice is friendly—they're playing Good Cop, Bad Cop, like in the movies, I decide—but he actually makes me feel even more nervous. He's definitely trying to trip me up and I keep my face hidden.

Good Cop goes on, "Now she's a blue roan cocker spaniel, isn't she? Lovely dogs. Had one myself once. What's her name?"

I look up and see Mum giving me "don't be so rude" looks from the sofa and now I'm scared of making her suspicious. It's exhausting trying to juggle about ten different personalities in the air at once.

"Trudy," I say in a steady sort of voice, hoping they might think I'm actually being friendly. Mum settles back on the sofa. Phew! One down, two to go.

"Well, have you and Trudy noticed anyone strange wandering around? We've seen evidence of someone sleeping on the beach by the yacht club."

I shrug casually.

"Come on, Alix. Speak up, you should always help the police," Mum chips in, and I glare at her. Does she have to treat me like a six-year-old, especially when I'm the adult around here most of the time now?

I don't know what to say and look down at Trudy again as Bad Cop barks out, "Maybe you and your friends had a campfire over the weekend?"

The less I say the better, I decide, so I say, "I haven't seen anything."

Mum frowns at me.

"What about in the shops maybe, or the post office?" says Good Cop. He's looking at me closely and I can see Mum's about to speak. I don't know if she's seen Samir and his family in town but I can't take any chances. If she mentions anything about them the police will be around there giving the whole family the third degree.

"Just the same old, same old. No one new."

There's a pause while we all stand looking at each other. Then Bad Cop says, "We're looking for illegal immigrants. We've had information that a boat is due around here this week, smugglers, bringing people over from France. They tip them out in the sea, leave them to it."

"They wouldn't last long in this weather," says Mum sympathetically, and I shoot her a grateful glance.

Then Good Cop says, "So you let us know if you see anything suspicious, Alix. We're relying on local people like you," and he gives me a big friendly smile.

I ask cautiously, "What would happen if you found one of these illegal immigrants?"

"You let us worry about that, love. We'll see ourselves out. Thank you, Mrs. Miller," and they're gone.

"Well, you weren't very helpful," says Mum, giving me her most annoyed look.

"I haven't seen anything," I snap back, and run upstairs to my room. I have to get ready for school and the bus leaves in twenty minutes.

But I feel totally freaked by the police visit and I go over to the window and stare out across the Solent, trying to calm down. The sea is quite rough today. The wind has turned around and it's tugging the surf onto the beach in great white rolls. It would be a terrific day to take a board out.

My hands are literally shaking. Am I completely insane or am I doing my bit? At Dunkirk, Grandpa just did what he was told and anyway it was pretty obvious who you were helping there. But how do I really know what sort of person Mohammed is? More to the point, how does Samir know?

When I turn back into the room my eye catches sight of the old scorecard from the last time I went bowling with Dad. It's pinned to my notice board with a dart I threw after he left.

Suddenly I want to see Dad more than anything else in the world. Tell him about Samir and Mohammed and ask him what I should do. Even though he never scores much above zero in our family.

Mum calls him a "waste of space." When I was little I thought she meant his job was packing boxes and he always left a bit of space in each box, so he got the sack for wasting space. But that wasn't the problem.

"Johnnie never stuck at anything," Mum would say. "He

just wanted to change me from being a punk into a boring housewife."

She always called Dad "Johnnie" when she was angry with him.

Then she'd give a sneery laugh and say, "That's why he went off with Gorgeous Gloria. She'll do anything he wants."

"He didn't need to change me," I would reply grumpily. But he still never contacts me; he's too busy enjoying himself with the Gremlin. And Mum doesn't seem to care. She never tries to find him. Or at least that's what she says. Is she better off without him? Am I?

Nine o'clock sounds on Radio 1 and now I'm seriously late for school and in a load of trouble with Spicer. But it's hard to think about school when everyone seems to be closing in on us. First Lindy finds the hut and Samir is terrified she'll tell Terrence and his gang about Mohammed. Then Mrs. Saddler questions me in the street and now the police turn up in our cottage. What will happen when they find out I've lied?

Let's hope I get to school before I get arrested.

22. Trumpet Steven

It's lunchtime. Kim's sitting on a bench by the basketball court with Steven and I'm sure they're playing Mozart in the air. I can almost recognize the fingering by now.

Steven's saying to Kim as I come over, "You'll only have to play the first bit."

Kim says, "I always mess up at the fourth bar."

"Try not to think about it." Steven's straightening his tie. He has a pink plastic lunch box on his knee and a thermos flask, like the fishermen on the beach. I could comb my hair in the reflection from his shoes.

"Hi, Ali," says Kim, smiling up at me. "Come and join us." But I've already spotted Samir shooting baskets on his own as usual. I want to tell him about the police visit and also that I'll be late getting to the hut tonight because I've got a thirty-minute detention for being late.

Then Lindy calls out from across the playground, "Hey, Two Percent, how's your cousin?"

The smile freezes on Kim's face and Samir lets the basketball roll away into the gutter, his face going dark with anger. I feel my fists clench.

Steven's voice rings out sort of deep and strong like when he blasts down his trumpet.

"His name's Samir, thank you very much." He sounds like one of the teachers.

But Lindy just flicks her hair back and walks over, squaring up to Steven who's still sitting on the bench.

"I don't think..." Kim starts up, but Steven just puts his hand on her shoulder and Kim stops abruptly.

"Who asked you?" says Lindy.

At least Terrence was permanently excluded last year, or we'd probably have his entire gang on us by now, like a pack of wolves. What if Lindy's already told Terrence about Mohammed and what if he finds out that Steven's mouthing off to her? There was an incident in a London school last week when a teenage gang broke in through the security gates, grabbed a fifteen-year-old boy in the detention hall and stabbed him in the back four times. He'd looked at the gang leader the wrong way in the street. Would Terrence do that if he thought we were being mean to his sister?

I want to warn Trumpet Steven to stick to Mozart, it's safer, but before I get the chance he's off again.

"People should be called by their proper names, don't you think?"

He sounds like the Prime Minister.

"No I don't, you muppet," Lindy sneers back. "Anyway, it's only a joke."

"Can you see anyone laughing?" There's a pause. No one says anything.

Then Steven says, "What do you mean 'Two Percent'?"

Lindy gives her meanest smile and says, "Ask them about Two Percent." Then she walks off.

"So what did she mean?" asks Steven coolly, opening his lunch box, which I'd rather die than be seen with.

"Nothing," says Kim quickly, looking around at me and Samir.

But Steven isn't in our form so he won't know about the lesson with Spicer last week.

"Our form teacher told us that only 2.7 percent of refugees ever get to Britain," I say, and Steven looks at me with interest, "so Lindy calls Samir 'Two Percent.' "

Steven takes a bite of his sandwich, tuna and cucumber on whole wheat—I've got a bag of crisps, no time to pack anything else—and then he says in his most thoughtful voice, "That's very offensive."

"Exactly," says Kim, "and Ali stands up to her when Lindy says that."

I go a bit red, I didn't really want Samir to know that but Samir is grinning at me and then he pulls a roll-up from behind his ear. He's never going to spark up out here!

Before I can say anything he says, "Got a light?"

Steven digs in his pocket and says, "Sure," and pulls out a disposable lighter.

Even Kim's mouth has dropped open.

But then Steven goes into the most awful coughing fit I've ever seen. I'm certain he's going to expire on the bench with his pink lunch box spilling everywhere. We stand around helplessly. I wonder if we should turn him upside down and thump him on the back but gradually he slows to a stop. "Chest infection," he splutters, and wipes his mouth on a handkerchief he takes out of his pocket. I catch sight of his initials, STG, embroidered on one corner. I don't think his mother's a punk.

"Steven, you don't smoke, do you?" Kim asks in a shocked voice. She hasn't blinked for about five minutes and her eyes are as big as Frisbees.

Steven's still coming up for air but after a minute he says, "No, I found the lighter in the music room. I thought it might come in useful."

Samir is halfway down the roll-up by now but he has the good sense to blow the smoke away from Steven. I'm looking around nervously for a teacher, of course, as I'm Number One Nerd of Year 10. Kim seems to be too bewildered to be worried, which is totally not like her.

Then Steven says, "I'm supposed to be on antibiotics, but I hate them, they make me sick, so I haven't started yet," and he pulls a box of pills out of his pocket.

We all yell out at the same time, "Antibiotics!"

We're thinking of Mohammed of course and what the druggist and Lindy said about infection.

Me and Kim do a high five and Samir grinds his cigarette end out on the tarmac.

Steven is staring around at us, his eyes still watery from the coughing fit. "You've lost me," he says.

Then Samir crouches down until he is at eye level with Steven and says, "How much for the pills?"

23. Worse

"You're joking," says Steven. It's the first time I've seen him looking off balance.

Samir looks up at me and those eyes are pleading again but there's nothing I can do. I mean, by now Steven has probably decided that Samir is some foreign drug dealer and I'm his postman or whatever, dropping pills around to users.

Kim starts to blink furiously and Steven says, "Something in your eye?" and he reaches out to her but she brushes his hand away.

"Just give him the pills, Steven. We're hiding an illegal immigrant and he's very sick."

I can't believe she said that! Neither can Samir. He throws himself to his feet, his ice man image in total meltdown, and starts shouting in Arabic. At least I recognize the language by now. He's roaring away, waving his arms about, pacing back and forward. His Arsenal scarf is swinging off his neck and he's scuffing his sneakers on the ground, tearing the hole in the toe into a great huge gash.

Charlie Parks and his football crowd arrive on the court and start jeering, "Hey, Two Percent's lost it!" One of them yells out, "Shut it, you Paki!"

Now half our class, the Jayne family and Lindy too, are gathered around the mesh fence, screaming with laughter, winding the boys up even more.

Before I can do anything Samir rushes Charlie, taking him completely by surprise, and punches him in the mouth. I can't help letting out a cheer and I hear Steven behind me call out, "Serves him right."

Samir's put up with enough rubbish this week and probably for months, maybe even years. Everyone thinks they can take a pop at him and his family just because they're refugees or Arabs or because they think Samir and his family are from Pakistan, which is stupid anyway, even if he was.

Mr. Spicer says there's no such word as "Paki," it's a made-up racist word.

"People from Pakistan are called Pakistani," he says, glaring around the class, and it makes me think he must know what Samir is called around the school. It would be nice if he actually did something about it.

Charlie is taller than Samir and he's quite stocky. He staggers back, blood pouring from his top lip, and then he throws himself at Samir and they roll on the ground, kicking and punching.

The football crowd circle them yelling, "Mash him, Charlie." I start to push my way through but three teachers suddenly appear, grab Samir and Charlie and haul them apart, dragging them off into school.

I call out, "It wasn't Samir's fault, sir," but they just ignore me.

Lindy yells through the fence, "They'll exclude him now," and the Jayne family shriek and clutch each other.

The football crowd go over to the fence and join in, looking over their shoulders at us and saying things really loudly like,

"Taliban had it coming" and "he needed a good kicking," as if Samir had just stood there letting Charlie beat him up.

But I'm really, really scared for him now. Naazim will be called to the school over the fight, and will they get into trouble because they're not English and what if they make Samir tell about Mohammed?

And then an even worse thought comes into my mind. What if Trumpet Steven goes to the police and tells them we are hiding an illegal immigrant? I mean, look at him, with his knotted tie and his briefcase and his posh mum in her designer suits. She's definitely the type to sneak to the police. Maybe she's waiting for Steven in the car park right now and they'll go off together and Mohammed will be behind bars in about one hour and ten minutes.

I turn around to look at Steven and Kim and I feel quite numb. Steven is packing his lunch away into his leather brief-case and brushing crumbs off his blazer as if nothing's happened, and Kim's busy sorting through her music bag, her hair covering her face like a mask. Doesn't she care? Maybe they've already agreed behind my back to go to the police or their mums? And I'm back to square one, as Grandpa used to say, wondering if I made a mistake telling Kim about Mohammed.

I feel so upset, I must have let out some sort of sob because Kim rushes up, throws her arms around me and gives me a big hug on tiptoe. "It's okay, Ali, don't worry. I've explained every-thing. He can help. Steven's cool."

"Is he?" I say suspiciously, and I push Kim away. Kim stares up at me, her eyes hurt and confused, and I feel as if I've sprinted off on the wrong foot.

Steven is clipping his briefcase shut and then he says, "Is there a problem?"

"How do I know I can trust you?" I say, and I can feel Kim tensing beside me.

But they have to understand how deadly serious this is and what's at stake here.

"Samir will be in massive trouble if you blab to your mum or the police," I say. "And Mohammed could get deported!" Steven straightens up, pulling at his tie, his briefcase tucked under his arm.

Then he says in this ultra serious voice, "What if I meet Mohammed after school today, okay?"

24. More than a Game of Football

But after school Steven's mum grabs him and he has to go home first. Me and Kim stay in town at the bus stop on the high street and I nearly bite my fingernails down to the elbows waiting for him to show up.

Kim keeps saying, "He won't say anything, Ali, promise. Steven has principles; he's always going on about justice and people in prison in China because they oppose their governments."

"Mohammed's on Hayling Island, not China," I mutter, checking my watch for the umpteenth time. "Where is he?"

Eventually Steven strolls up. He's dressed in a neatly pressed denim jacket and jeans, but at least he's alone.

"Did you say anything?" I almost yell at him.

I'm expecting police cars to converge on the bus station from all sides, sirens blaring, like in American cop shows.

But Steven gives me a look that could wither the sun and says, "What do you take me for?"

"Okay," I mutter, and we get on the bus.

Kim and Steven climb straight upstairs, laughing away like a couple of kids on an outing. The top of the bus is empty and they go right to the back and sit down close together.

They probably want to practice their Mozart fingering, I decide, so I go up front and sit on my own.

I have to admit it's good to have some time to myself to think. So much has happened today. But apart from all the stuff with the police and the fight and now another person involved in our massive secret, something else happened this morning that has been lurking around in the back of my mind.

Just before I dashed out of the house, already late for school because I'd spent ages upstairs after the police had gone, Mum had called from the living room, "Alexandra."

"What!" I'd yelled back impatiently.

She didn't answer, so I stomped in, moaning at being made even more late.

Mum was sort of tucked under a blanket, breakfast telly blaring out.

"Sausages for dinner?" she said.

"Whatever," I muttered, annoyed she had held me back for such a stupid reason and then I ran off.

But now when I think about it, Mum's face was all smudged and bleary as though she'd been crying. If she has, shouldn't I be going back home instead of charging off to our man? And I'm skipping detention with Mr. Spicer this evening. I'd already decided there was no way I was going to detention, leaving Kim to take Steven to the hut. Samir would go ballistic.

I wonder why my mum was crying. Is it because of Grandpa? Or maybe my "waste of space" Dad? Or maybe it's something I've done to her, like how I behaved when the police came around. And I'm just deciding that of course it's because of me, I mean let's face it I'm not exactly Daughter of the Year at the moment, yelling at her about Dad and hiding stuff from her, when the bus stops at Sandy Point.

After the bright sunshine yesterday, today is cold, gray and miserable again. It rained quite a lot this morning and the path over the marsh to the Lifeboat Station is almost under water. There are a couple of yachts tacking to and fro out on the Solent but the yacht club road is deserted like most Mondays in winter.

Steven is picking his way gingerly through the mud. He's still wearing his shiny school shoes.

Kim's back in her fantasy world of Mozart, humming to herself, and I'm getting totally worked up about how Samir is going to react when I turn up with another school friend.

So I'm not really concentrating when I turn around the side of the Lifeboat Station. The beach below the piles of breakwater pebbles is mostly deserted. But down by the pillbox I can see two figures, one standing, one leaning against the old concrete wall. Its takes me a couple of seconds to realize why they look so familiar.

Its Samir and Mohammed!

"There they are," says Kim cheerfully, and she pulls Steven down the pebbles. I try to sprint ahead to get there first but I slip and I'm too late. By the time I arrive Samir is scuffing his torn sneakers in the sand and winding his Arsenal scarf around his neck, glaring at Steven.

"Just listen, Samir, please," Kim is saying. "Steven's all right, he's safe, he's not going to run to the police or his parents, are you, Steve?" and she pulls on Steven's arm, as if to encourage him.

Steven's face is impassive. He is watching Mohammed carefully and as usual Mohammed's head is bent, his eyes and face hidden, his scruffy hair sticking out from under a black beanie hat, which Samir must have given him.

"What are you doing out here? Someone might see you," I say nervously to Samir, but he doesn't answer me, his eyes are fixed on Steven.

Any minute now someone is going to kick off again, and if it's me I don't think even Kim will be able to cool me down.

Then Steven says to Samir, "You support Arsenal?" Silence from the ice man.

"Do you think they'll win the League?" says Steven, and Samir shrugs.

Mohammed raises his head, his face wary. The wound on his forehead, above his bruised eye, looks very hot and red, and sort of green around the edges. Samir said the smugglers hit him with a baseball bat before they chucked him overboard. I can't help wondering if Steven brought the antibiotics with him, but it doesn't seem the right moment to ask.

Mohammed starts speaking in a low voice and I can make out the words "...football...Iraq...win..." mixed in with Arabic. Samir gives a sort of scornful laugh, and they're both looking at us in a funny, peculiar way. Kim signals to me with her eyes and I raise my eyebrows back. Now what's going on?

Then Samir says, "Arsenal's a great team, but we support the Iraqi football team, the Lions of Mesopotamia," and his voice sounds all sort of proud.

He says something quickly to Mohammed. It sounds a bit like "ammo," does that mean ammunition? I decide to ask. "Ammo what?"

Samir laughs more gently. "Ammo Baba," he says. "He's our greatest footballer, like the Pelé of Iraqi football." Mohammed nods and snorts in agreement.

"Last summer we beat Saudi Arabia one-nothing and we won the Asian cup," Samir goes on. "The whole of Baghdad went crazy. People were running through the streets waving flags, and some of them were even firing guns in the air. It was on the news. Me and Naazim and Auntie Selma were jumping up and down so much the Chinese below were knocking on the ceiling." And Samir gives a big grin.

"We saw it on TV," says Steven, which really catches me by surprise. How does he know stuff like that? "It was really cool. My mum and dad said maybe it'd be a new beginning for Iraq."

I can't imagine snooty Steven's mum worrying about Iraq's future. But then what do I know? I thought Chaz was cool and look how he turned out, and then I thought Kim was racist. How wrong was that? So much for relying on my own judgments.

But Samir says something to Mohammed and they are both looking at Steven in a more sort of curious way, which is better than open hostility.

Then Steven gets the box of pills out of his pocket and offers them to Mohammed. This doesn't go down too well. Mohammed shrinks away as if he's scared, and he starts waving one arm around and saying, "No, no."

"He thinks you're offering him drugs," says Samir, and says something in Arabic to Mohammed.

I can't help grinning. Geeky Steven with the pressed jeans and Toyota mum, pushing drugs on Hayling beach. Well, he is, of course, only they're just antibiotics.

Samir and Mohammed talk some more and then Mohammed reaches out and takes the pills.

"Zank you," he says, raising his eyes and looking up at us for the first time.

And then we have one of those embarrassing moments when no one knows what to say next. Everyone goes dead silent, and all you can hear are the gulls screaming and the sea dragging back and forth over the sand. Samir has turned and he's staring out to sea, all frozen up again. Mohammed has tucked back into himself. I can see Kim is standing very close to Steven and I'm just wondering if I've missed something when there's a hooting and whistling and we all turn, startled.

It's Terrence Bellows and he's got blond Gaz with him, the biggest thug in Terrence's gang. What has Lindy gone and done?

25. Not So Brave

Terrence and Gaz swagger over, their baggy jeans halfway down their hips, jackets wide open, fists clenched by their sides. They're grinning like apes showing off their teeth and you can see they think they've won the lottery or something.

"Bingo!" yells Terrence, and Gaz gives out a really nasty laugh. "Bloody United Nations just swam in. What you monkeys doing hanging around my gaff?" And he slaps the side of the pillbox. Lindy must have blabbed to him, otherwise what is he doing all the way down here?

He suddenly shoves Samir hard to one side so he falls into Steven and Kim, almost tripping them over. Blond Gaz makes a move toward me and I step back, my feet skidding on the wet sand.

I'm terrified, so what is everyone else feeling?

Then Terrence reaches down and rips Mohammed's hat off his head. Mohammed cowers down.

"Mate, we're being overrun," he roars to blond Gaz. "Hundreds of 'em, and you muppets," he points what looks like a flick knife at me and Kim and Steven, "should be thinking about your own people instead of hanging around with this scum."

He snorts back and then lands a huge gob of spit on Mohammed's head. Gaz laughs like a drain, as Grandpa used to say.

I'm looking around desperately for Trudy to rescue me. But I haven't been home yet so of course she's not here. What are we going to do if these two set on us?

"We don't want any trouble," says Steven in his BBC English, which just makes the thugs hoot even louder. Steven's face is deathly white, and he's put his arm around Kim who looks like she's shrunk even smaller.

I reach in my pocket for my cell phone and wonder if I can dial the police without removing it, but even if I could there's no signal down on the beach. By the time we even hear the sirens, which could take ages to get down the Island, we'd be mincemeat and the thugs long gone. Anyway, I'm not sure if I want Good Cop and Bad Cop turning up now. We're breaking the law ourselves, aren't we?

Terrence and Gaz are throwing the woolly hat between them, yelling, "Come and get it, Taliban."

Mohammed has raised his head slightly and Samir says something to him in Arabic. "What you gibbering about, you monkeys?" mocks Terrence. Gaz starts burbling nonsense words, which makes the two of them laugh even harder.

How dumb can you get? I'm beginning to get really, really angry and I can feel myself tensing, ready to leap at one of them and to hell with the consequences. Kim is already reaching out a steadying hand toward me when Mohammed stands up.

He's quite tall when he straightens, and as he squares his shoulders the thugs take a step backward like Lindy did in the hut. They're not so brave now.

A steady stream of Arabic is coming from Samir and it sounds as though he's pleading with Mohammed.

"Mate," says Gaz, "time to go, eh? Looks like he's gonna throw a bomb or something."

I wish, I can't help thinking.

"I'm not scared of him," snarls Terrence, and with a sudden movement he flicks open the blade of the knife.

I hear Kim gasp beside me and I freeze on the spot. Now what are we going to do?

Samir is reaching out to Mohammed but Mohammed takes a step sideways and roars out in a massive terrifying voice, "No more!"

He whirls around, kicking out his right foot, like something out of a Kung Fu movie.

His foot slams into some empty beer bottles standing on a rock. The bottles rocket into the air and smash against the concrete wall of the pillbox, splintering glass toward Terrence and Gaz.

They both duck and throw their arms up as shards of glass rain down on them.

Wow! I think, that's finished them, but Terrence still has the knife and he jabs it toward Mohammed. I get a sudden ghastly picture of blood spurting from his stomach.

I'm about to lunge forward when Mohammed kicks the knife so sweetly that Terrence's hand flies open and the knife drops onto the wet sand. Terrence lets out a cry of pain. "I'm outta here," Gaz says in a shaky voice.

"Wait for me," yells Terrence, and they both take off running and stumbling back up the mound of breakwater pebbles, swearing back at Mohammed over their shoulders.

At the top Terrence stops for a second and yells out, "This ain't over," and he makes a rude gesture.

Then they disappear.

We all let out a sigh of relief.

"That is very good, they go away now," says Mohammed, and it's the first time I've heard him speak so clearly.

It feels a bit weird; I thought he only knew a few words. It makes me feel very suspicious again just as I was beginning to trust him.

What do I really know about our man and what he's doing here?

But before I can say anything Steven says in his grown-up voice, "I didn't know you spoke English."

Mohammed nods and rubs a hand across his face. "I learn some in the university. My brother, he is better, he is very, very good."

I look across to Samir and he says to me and Steven, "Mohammed and his brother were interpreters for the British army in Basra. The army couldn't have coped without people like them."

"I see," I say, but Samir can see I'm suspicious. He tries to fix me with that pleading look but I give a slight shake of my head.

Mohammed says, "I know English, but not good and then the men hit my head and it is hurt. The sea gives me so cold and I feel very sick. I cannot think..." He says something in Arabic to Samir.

"Mohammed was very confused when we found him. It was difficult for him to think clearly and remember his English. It's only coming back slowly," Samir says. He takes a step toward me. "Alix?" he says, but I don't reply.

No one says anything for a minute. Then Mohammed says in a tired voice, "I come to England to ask your queen to help me."

"That might be a bit difficult," says Steven, and he gives Kim a squeeze.

Kim's eyes are wide as saucers.

"She is a good queen," says Mohammed more firmly, "and she must listen. I tell her I work hard to keep her soldiers safe. Dangerous work. You understand?" He looks around at us with such desperation and fear.

"You must to understand, you are helping me, all of you, and now I need your queen to help me. I cannot go back. They have kill my brother and they will kill me." He slumps to the ground exhausted.

There's a shocked silence except for the gulls wheeling and crying overhead. Kim has buried her face in Steven's jacket and Samir is staring out to sea, frozen like an ice man.

But Steven isn't looking convinced. "So where did you learn martial arts?" he says.

Mohammed is silent, his head slumped onto his chest. Say something, I think. Now's your chance to convince us all, and then with a sudden stab of fear I think, Did I get this all wrong? Maybe he's been fooling us all along and he's really a trained terrorist come over here to bomb us to death.

Samir turns and we stare straight into each other's eyes. His face is strained and tense. Is he scared he's made a terrible mistake too?

Then Mohammed lifts his head and his eyes are dulled with pain. "I learn in university," he says in such a quiet voice we all lean forward to catch his words. "I am best at kickboxing, I win all the..."—he mutters a word in Arabic that sounds like *jahwize* and stares up at Samir.

"Prizes," says Samir. "He was the best in his year at martial arts. That's all," and his face relaxes with relief. He pats Mohammed gently on the back.

"He's a peaceful man, aren't you, my friend?" Mohammed nods briefly and lets his head drop again.

I hesitate and I can almost feel Samir's eyes boring into me. This is not the time to make a mistake, and then I remember asking Grandpa just before he died, "How did you know you did the right thing, going to France? You could have been killed."

"Gut feeling," he told me. "It felt right and off I went." Right now I feel in my gut that Mohammed is a good person.

I say in a clear voice, "I believe him."

There's a general mutter and everyone relaxes and then I say, "The trouble is, the police came to my house this morning and..."

"The police?" Samir and Kim and Steven all yell out at the same time.

So how come I'm always the one who ends up in trouble?

26. More Trouble?

Steven's looking worried. He obviously didn't bargain for this when he said he'd come and meet Mohammed.

I tell them what happened before school. "So the police are already alerted. Now do you see why he has to stay in the hut all the time?"

Everyone nods, even Mohammed.

"What about that refugee group you said could help him?" I say to Samir.

"I haven't had time to get on the Internet in the library," Samir says with a shake of his head.

Then Steven says thoughtfully, "My mum knows a bit about refugee organizations…"

"*Your* mum?" I interrupt, and then I shut my mouth. Steven glares at me and I feel as though I'm in the principal's office or something.

"What's the problem?" he says.

"She always looks so…" Posh, I think, but I don't want to say that out loud.

Kim shuffles a bit closer to Steven, and Samir has an arm under Mohammed's shoulders, heaving him up. No one's standing near me. "Do you always judge people by appearances?" says Steven in that cool voice.

That's exactly what racists do, isn't it? Kim is looking up at me and then at Steven with this sort of confused look on her face. I go bright red and mumble a sort of apology, feeling really small.

"Anyway," goes on Steven, "I'm not going to tell Mum anything, it's just that she's a useful resource." He makes her sound like a search engine on the Web.

We help Mohammed back to the hut and Samir says, "I had to leave my last school because of racist bullies like Terrence. I can't keep changing schools."

Steven says, "You're not going anywhere, Samir. You have friends at Park Road," and Mohammed repeats "friends" in a low mutter, as we all nod in agreement.

We walk together to the bus stop and Steven's got his arm around Kim again. How did I miss that? Geeky Steven and my best friend—an item? Even though he's a bit geeky, I feel happy for Kim. "Way to go, kid!" as Dad would say when he did his American accent.

Mum's in the kitchen when I get home and as Trudy jumps up at me, desperate for a walk, Mum says, "You're late; I was going to start on the sausages."

She looks miserable, as if that's anything new, but then she says in this really slow and sort of strange voice, "Where have you been this time?"

This time, what does she mean by that?

"I had a detention, the police coming this morning, they made me late for school." Excellent. I skipped the detention. Yet another lie.

Mum snorts loudly and says, "Mr. Spicer wouldn't give you a detention for being late just the once."

Actually he would, he's that mean, but all the parents think he's wonderful because he wears a suit.

"So what have you really been up to, Alexandra?" and she stares at me with this totally suspicious look.

"Nothing, Mum, I don't know what you mean."

"Just because I'm stuck here at home all day," she starts ranting on, "doesn't mean you can just do whatever you want and come in all hours."

She's riffling through cupboards and the fridge, still leaning on her crutches, but she does seem more steady on her feet. "We seem to have gone through an awful lot of food this week."

"Lots of people keep coming around, don't they?" I say, quickly hiding my face as I open a can of dog food for Trudy. But I can feel myself getting all hot and bothered so I try to change the subject. "Do you know Steven Goddard's mum?"

"Mmm, she does coffee mornings," says Mum, absently staring at the last few slices of bread. "Charity stuff, for refugees I think, or is it the homeless?"

She's going through the fridge again and she pulls out a full pack of bacon and the sausages. "Well, I suppose we won't starve."

"What's she like?" I ask, still bending over Trudy's dish.

"Val Goddard? Total nutcase," says Mum. "Always campaigning for something and you wouldn't think it—all those smart little suits and her leather briefcase. She's a personal adviser in a bank, you know. "

So I'm not the only one who judges by appearances.

And then she cracks a smile, about the first one I've seen this millennium, and says, "It's nice having people drop in." For a second it feels a bit like the old times when Mum and me just used to have fun together. When did things begin to change? It's like everything has sneaked up on us, Dad running off and leaving us like welfare cases and then Grandpa dying. I didn't realize how old he really was, I thought he'd just go on forever. And then Mum breaking her leg and going completely horrible.

And now my big fat secret is hanging in the air between us, like a bloated belly. I hate all the lies and taking food without asking, even though I actually pay for stuff around here these days, well, I give Mum eight pounds a week. But I know she's been getting Bert to help her with benefit forms so we must be really short of money. I feel like Oliver Twist, on the verge of being thrown in the workhouse. Grandpa never claimed any benefits, did he?

But Mum is a tad more cheerful when other people are around. She loved all the attention from Bert and Kevin and Kim and even the police.

"We'll just have to invite more people over then, won't we?" I grin, and I give her a hug for the first time in ages. And it's so scary. She feels like a midget in my arms. It's as though I've grown taller, like I'm sitting on an elephant or something and I've outgrown my own mum and the cottage. My whole life. When did that happen?

Mum clings to me for a minute and I smell her Passion Fruit facial scrub from the Body Shop, which I always give her at Christmas.

Then she pulls away and snaps, "I don't know what you're up to, my girl, but if you get another detention I'll ground you."

I feel myself beginning to get all angry and upset again but I manage to persuade myself to keep calm. I need to keep Mum happy at the moment until things are sorted out with our man.

So I say, "Sorry, look, why don't you go online and do some shopping? Fill up the fridge in case we have some more unexpected visitors, and I'll make dinner?"

"I suppose so," she grumbles, and she stomps off into the

living room on her crutches. Our computer's on a desk next to the TV. I use it for my homework and Mum uses it mainly to email Uncle Peter in New York.

I hear the computer booting up and call out, "Order some hummus and pita bread."

"Ooh, going all healthy on me now." Mum laughs. "Anything else you fancy?"

"Loads of bread and cheese, then we can make everyone sandwiches, right?"

She doesn't say anything but I can hear her tapping away furiously so I relax and put on the sausages.

"We had hummus and pita bread every day at home," Samir had said on the beach, when he was remembering all about his life in Iraq, the life he misses so much it's turned him to ice. "And in our garden we didn't have roses and apple trees. We had orange trees and one lemon tree."

"Wow," I said. "Fresh oranges every day."

"Only in winter," said Samir. "But the best was the red watermelon. I used to help my mum bring it home from the *Shorjah* market. I always moaned about going shopping with her. I wanted to go out and play with Daoud. I'd give anything to be able to go shopping with my mum again."

It was another one of those tricky moments, so I said, "Do you get snow in Iraq?"

"No. I've never seen snow," he said. "But you wouldn't stand the heat in summer. It gets up to fifty degrees or more, even. You'd go mad."

"Didn't you have air-conditioning?"

Samir throws me a scornful look. "Of course. But the best times were when we were allowed to sleep on the roof, like my grandparents always did before air-conditioning. Me and

Naazim used to lie awake all night counting stars. Some people keep pigeons on their roofs in bamboo cages and you would hear them cooing all night."

"Bit like camping."

"Except you don't need a tent, it's so hot."

"You see the best stars on cold winter nights here. But you couldn't sleep on the beach in winter," I said.

"I wouldn't sleep on a British beach in summer!" Samir laughed.

Sleeping on the roof—they must have flat roofs in Baghdad—seeing all the stars, listening to the pigeons, eating red watermelon made me want to jump on a plane and see for myself.

"It sounds amazing. I'd love to sleep out on the roof. Maybe the school will organize a trip when everything settles down."

"People have tried sleeping on their roofs again. The air-conditioning keeps shutting off because the electricity supply is so bad. But it's very dangerous. Uncle Sayeed said the neighbor's little girl was killed by a stray bullet coming across the roof last summer. She was only four."

There was a long pause and I didn't know what to say. But then Samir said, "Sometimes I think we will never go home."

But never is a long time, Grandpa used to say.

I've laid the table properly for once. I'm sick of crouching in front of the telly, well, I'm sick of the telly really. I'm just about to call Mum into the kitchen for dinner when the house phone goes. I go to answer it but Mum has already picked up. It could be Kim because my cell phone is dead and maybe she's got some news from Steven, so I go into the living room, but as soon as Mum sees me she clicks off and turns back quickly to the computer.

But not before I've seen this dead guilty look on her face. So I'm not the only one hiding stuff in this house, am I?

27. More Pants

I can't face Chaz the next morning; it feels like I'm betraying Mohammed and Samir just walking into his stinking shop. So I skip my paper route and instead decide to go and take Mohammed breakfast early. It was so cold last night, there was ice on the inside of my window when I woke up, so what must it be like in the hut?

Mum is still asleep so Trudy and me manage to sneak out of the house with all the supplies. Poor Trudy has hardly had a decent walk since Saturday; I swear if she could speak she'd be on the phone to the Humane Society about me. It's very cold outside and barely daylight. The Island is so mysterious this early on a winter morning. Sometimes, walking out with Grandpa, who always got up at six, we'd tramp right along the inlet to the sand flats beyond the yacht club. All the oystercatchers and gulls and Brent geese out hunting for food, not a boat on the water. It can feel like the far end of the world out there sometimes. So lonely when the fog is really thick, even quite scary, especially now without Grandpa.

It makes me think about how Mohammed must have felt when they threw him into the sea in the fog. The water was so cold and deep and he wouldn't have been able to see the shore.

It must have been completely terrifying and he must have felt so alone and so helpless.

I'm thinking all these thoughts and jogging down the road when a small blue van pulls up on the other side. The driver gives a honk and I look across. It says *Blacks and Son Medical Supplies* in red lettering on the side of the van. I'm thinking maybe it's someone who's lost when the driver gets out.

Oh my God! It's Dad!

And all I can think about is the armful of supplies I've got for my asylum seeker. My knees go weak with terror. We're finished now. But Dad's here. After all this time.

I don't know what to do. I really just want to run across the road and fling my arms around him, but also I want to yell at him, "Where have you been for like two years?!"

I just stand there shifting the load in my arms and it's Trudy who breaks the ice, rushing over and snuffling around his feet.

He bends down and gives her a pat saying, "Good girl, you know who I am, don't you, old girl?" Then he straightens and says, "How about a hug, Alix?"

Bad timing, Dad. I can't believe I'm thinking this, but I have to keep our secret from him, don't I?

Dad crosses over and puts his arms around me and all the packs of sandwiches and the flask of coffee and the hot-water bottle, which fortunately is hidden in a carrier bag because that would look totally weird, and I'm sort of suffocated with all this stuff pushing into my chest as Dad gives me an elephant type of hug. But he smells the same—Lynx aftershave and the sweat from his armpits, and his bony old arms feel the same and it's so good to see him. Just not exactly at this moment.

I pull away after a minute and say awkwardly, "What are you doing here?"

"Your mum called me," he says as though that happens like every day.

What? Mum has his phone number! And she's been ringing him behind my back! That's why she looked so shifty yesterday.

"She said she didn't know how to get hold of you," I say. So who's lying now, I can't help thinking.

Dad shrugs but at least he looks a bit embarrassed. "Well, she should have told you. Anyway, we haven't been in touch that much. It's a bit difficult with Gloria."

What's she got to do with it? But I don't say anything, I don't trust myself to speak.

Then he says, "Your mum rang because she's worried about you. She thinks you're running wild. Is it a boy, Ali?" I let out a snort and think, Wish it was that simple. But you know how it is with me. I forget the silent button.

Dad is staring at me and then he notices that I'm not exactly carrying a load of schoolbooks.

"What's all this stuff?" he says, and he's eyeing me really suspiciously.

As I stare back I see that his hair is beginning to go gray at the sides like Kevin's, Kim's dad. It's still quite dark on top and Dad's cut it really short, which makes his ears stick out. But he's still got the same old pointy nose. When I was little I used to call him Pinocchio and he called me Snow White because I could eat four apples in one evening.

"It's just my school lunch," I say lamely. At least I'm wearing my uniform, but I have to get away from him before he asks too many questions even though he's only just turned up again.

"Look, Dad," I say nervously, "I'm going to be late and..." but I don't get time to finish.

Dad's cell phone starts ringing out the tune to *LA Law*. We used to watch that together. He flips it open and frowns.

"It's my boss," he says, and then he talks into the phone in a bored voice. "Yeah, yeah, I'm nearly at the hospital..."

What hospital? There isn't one on the Island. And is that a good way to speak to your boss?

"...no, there was an accident on the highway...no worries, I'll be there in five," and he flips off.

"Gotta go, doll. Ring me and we'll go bowling in our pants, eh?" And he shoves a piece of paper in my hand, gets back in the van and roars off.

What the hell is going on? I want to yell after him.

Dad hadn't really disappeared; Mum knew where he was all along and he wasn't even that far away! And now, when it suits her, she's decided to get him over to have a go at me. Just because she can't be bothered herself. Too wrapped up in her leg.

All the times I begged her to find him and she just shrugged as if it didn't matter and went off to write her stupid poetry.

I can feel tears welling up in my eyes as I watch the van swerve around the bend. What if I don't see him again for another two years? I look at the paper; it's just a cell phone number, no address or even a note or anything.

Why should I ring him? I can't bring myself to throw the paper away, so I shove it in my jacket pocket and stumble off, my cheeks wet with tears.

It feels weird going to the hut on my own. I almost turn back. I wish Kim or Samir or even Trumpet Steven was here.

I don't know what to say to Mohammed on my own. I hope he doesn't notice I've been crying. But Mohammed seems to take it all in his stride, emptying his old water bottle out the window and collecting all the rubbish in one bag for me to take home.

"Zank you, Aleex," he keeps saying. "Food and coffee is very good."

If he's seen my red eyes he's not saying anything. How do I explain I'm crying over seeing my dad when he probably won't ever see his family again? Like Samir. But somehow that doesn't make me feel any better.

"Have you started on the antibiotics?" I ask, and Mohammed nods.

So maybe he'll start to get better, I'm thinking, and then he can move on. My life just got mega complicated with Dad showing up like that and it's going to be harder and harder to keep all this hushed up.

"Do you learn Arabic in school?" Mohammed asks, breaking into my thoughts.

"No. French and German."

"I teach you," he says. "Tell Samir *shukran*, it mean 'thank you.' It will be surprise."

I repeat *shukran* about a hundred times until Mohammed is satisfied and then I give him an old Casio digital watch I found at the back of one of my drawers. He's delighted and keeps saying *shukran* and pressing the button, which lights up the dial in fluorescent green.

I tell him I'll be back about four with Samir, and then dash home to drop Trudy off and catch the bus to school.

I get to class just as the buzzer sounds and then I get my first piece of luck of the day. Spicer is off sick and Miss Redding, the sobbing student teacher, is taking our class roll call.

So I won't get into more trouble for cutting detention last night. Yay!

Lindy's already got her claws into the student teacher so no one notices me, except Kim, as I slip into the seat next to her.

I'm just about to tell her about Dad showing up when she whispers, "Steven's skipping school!"

Her eyes are staring into mine without blinking.

28. Speaking Arabic

Well, that must be a first, I'm thinking, and I'm really quite shocked.

"He's told his mum his chest hurts again and she's let him stay home. He's searching the Internet right now for refugee organizations," says Kim, and she still hasn't blinked.

Trumpet Steven playing hooky? Unbelievable. But I realize this is a big moment for Kim and say nothing. I try not to think much either, just in case.

Samir is excluded today and somehow it feels really weird without him. But it's Lindy I'm after, she betrayed us and she's not going to get away with it. At lunchtime I go looking for her.

"Watch out for her disgusting nail," says Kim as she hurries to keep up with me, but right now I don't care.

I find Lindy in the toilets and call out, "You told Terrence, didn't you?"

"You what?" says Lindy in a bored voice but I can see she's unfurling the nail.

"Leave it, Ali," says Kim, pulling at my sleeve, but I can't. It's been going around and around in my head, driving me crazy.

"He turned up on the beach with Gaz and threatened us with a knife. You couldn't keep it secret, could you? You had to tell Terrence about the hut. You set him on Samir just like a dog," I snarl at Lindy.

She's sorting out her gross hair in the mirror and pouting her lips like she's some sort of supermodel. I feel the anger and irritation rising and I'm about to start on her again when she says, "I told him nothing. I don't care about Two Percent or his so-called cousin."

"So why was Terrence all the way down Hayling Island yesterday?" And I feel like slapping her smug face but Kim's got me almost in a half nelson by now.

Lindy shrugs. "He's got to go somewhere, the police move him on from town," she says as she walks toward the door. "You need to get a life instead of hanging around with even more losers."

Kim has band practice all afternoon until about six, so I walk out the gates after school on my own with Lindy's words still going around in my head. I want to yell into her face, "I had a life, a perfectly good life, and then my dad skipped off, my grandpa died, my mum broke her leg and a completely illegal person turned up on my beach."

I haven't been to marathon training for a week and the coach has given up leaving messages on my cell phone. The last one said, *1 more chance.*

I really miss training, but even if I win, I don't need to get interviewed in the local paper anymore. Dad hasn't disappeared and I've got his number, not that I ever want to speak to him again.

I don't want to go home right now because if I do I expect I'll just have another fight with Mum, so I decide to go around to Samir's flat. We can go on the bus to the Island together to see Mohammed.

I ring the bell and have to wait a minute or two while Samir runs down. When he opens the door he says quickly, "Don't ask about the photos," which is a weird sort of welcome. Then he races up the narrow flight of stairs ahead of me and into the flat, which smells all warm and spicy.

"In here," says Samir, and he pulls me into the kitchen.

A short woman, her head completely covered in a black head scarf, is laying out sheets of incredibly thin pastry onto a huge tray on the kitchen table.

She's younger than Mum, in her thirties maybe, with the same light-brown skin as Samir, and she's wearing a full-length dark blue dress, a black cardigan and red slippers.

"Hello, Samir friend, good, sit, sit," and she gives me a huge smile and pushes me onto a stool.

"This is Auntie Selma," says Samir, grinning. "Hello," I say.

Auntie Selma speaks in rapid, heavily accented English, and it's hard to follow everything she says. But she and Samir hoot with laughter when I carefully say *shukran*.

"Where'd you learn that?" says Samir in surprise.

"Guess," and I give him a wink. Then I say, "What are you making?" I point to the jars of honey and bowls of mixture that look like nuts or perhaps garden gravel ground up quite small.

"Baklava," says Auntie Selma, and she and Samir have to say it about ten times before I get it.

That was the word I got wrong the last time I came to Samir's home. I thought they were making balaclavas for suicide bombers. How embarrassing. For a minute I can't meet Samir's eyes.

But that's not the only thing I got wrong in the last few days. I didn't realize that Mum and Dad have been speaking to each other for the last two years behind my back. That's so like sneaky of them and then I have an awful thought. Maybe

Mum thinks I don't deserve to be in touch with Dad because I'm "running wild" or whatever.

Samir is telling me that baklava is a kind of very sweet Middle Eastern pastry. Auntie Selma makes it by the tray load for the Turkish restaurant on the high street. "They pay her," he says, and I nod.

Every little helps, I think, like my paper route money. Although I've decided to quit so now I'm unemployed again. Can't wait to tell Mum the good news. She's bound to blame me.

Auntie Selma gives me two different kinds of pastries to try, and it's the most fantastic melt-in-your-mouth stuff I've ever had.

"Take, Alix," says Auntie Selma, and she hands me a spoon and a bowl of mixture. "Put here and here and we make together and make good, *inshallah*."

I look at Samir and he says, "*Inshallah*, it means God willing."

I try it out a couple of times and Auntie Selma corrects me until I get it right.

"*Shukran, inshallah*, I'm speaking Arabic," and I laugh. Auntie Selma laughs too, and says, "Alix make good Iraqi girl."

What would Auntie Selma think about hiding Mohammed? Maybe she would think we were crazy and tell us to go to the police. Is that what a good Iraqi girl would do?

We all work together for a while and it's really great fun. Samir and me get sticky to our elbows and then Samir gets a bottle of cola out of the fridge and, handing me a couple of plastic beakers, says, "Let's go next door. It's too hot in here."

He says something in Arabic to Auntie Selma and she smiles and waves us away. But as we leave the kitchen I suddenly think, What if Nasty Naazim is in the next room? I'm beginning to feel very nervous.

29. The Photos

Samir leads me into the living room. It's a small, square room with brightly colored cotton rugs on the tatty carpet and pieces of deep red velvety material thrown over the sofa and armchairs. No sign of Naazim, which is a relief.

But it feels as though I've stepped into a foreign country with all the colors and the sweet spicy smell floating in from the kitchen. Very different from our living room in the cottage with its wooden beams in the ceiling and the dark, polished furniture.

My eye is caught by the sideboard, which runs down one side of the room. It's absolutely crammed with dozens of photos of what look like family members and, even more incredible, the entire wall's covered in photos too. You can't see one square millimeter of wallpaper. I look over at Samir, who's fiddling with the radio, finding a music channel. I can tell by the way he's standing that he's embarrassed.

I look back at the photos of men and women, all ages, in groups and pairs and on their own, eating meals outdoors in white-hot sunlight. There are little children grinning with their front teeth missing and women with their hair covered, stirring big pans of food. These photos must be from Iraq.

"So where are you?" I say.

"It's not my family. It's Auntie Selma's, my uncle Sayeed's

wife. She came to England six months after me. Uncle Sayeed won't leave Iraq, so she cries about him a lot," says Samir over his shoulder.

"But the photos, are they all your auntie's family?" I say, astonished. How could anyone have so much family? "Where's your auntie?"

Samir points to a little girl of about nine with a ribbon in her curly hair, holding the hand of a man. He has a mustache and he's wearing some kind of long white tunic. "That's Auntie Selma with her father."

"What happened after that, did they lose the camera?" I say, grinning.

"No, everyone in these pictures is dead. Only Auntie Selma's left."

Samir's looking at me and then he drops his eyes as he sees my face change.

How could so many people from one family have died? Did they all get some terrible disease? Saddam Hussein couldn't have killed them all in his prisons, could he?

"I don't understand," I say.

Samir goes to the door and checks that Auntie Selma's busy. "She gets upset if we talk about it," he says, coming back and slumping down on the sofa. "Me and Naazim don't like it when she cries. We don't know what to do."

I sit down too, next to a table with a large, heavy book on it, covered with a green cloth.

"Auntie Selma comes from a village called Halabjah in the north of Iraq," Samir says. "It's where the Kurds live. They rebelled against Saddam Hussein and out of revenge he dropped gas bombs on the Kurdish villages. The worst attack was on one single day in 1988 when five thousand people were killed in Auntie Selma's village. Auntie Selma is the only one left in her family."

"It must have been a very big family," I say, thinking about Kim and all her brothers and sisters and uncles and cousins. Not like me, with just Mum.

Samir nods and such a sad look crosses his face.

"Yes," he says very quietly, and a chill goes through me. "Thousands and thousands of people were killed, and most of them were women and children. Naazim said he saw one picture of a man sitting over the bodies of his wife and ten children, all dead." Samir looks at me with his sad, dark eyes and I just stare back.

All that in this little living room, every day.

"Naazim doesn't let me look at those pictures, all those piles of dead bodies. Like they showed us in History class."

"Germany in World War II?" I say, and Samir nods. Grandpa's war, I think, only he didn't go to any concentration camps.

We are quiet for a few minutes. Samir goes back to fiddling with the radio and I look at the pictures on the wall.

Then I say, "But five thousand people killed from one bomb? Surely one bomb can't do that."

"No, there were hundreds of bombs, filled with horrific stuff like cyanide and mustard gas..."

"Gas? They used that in the trenches." Grandpa told me how his uncle Ted was gassed in World War I. He never worked again because his lungs were destroyed.

When Grandpa was a boy he used to wave a newspaper up and down in front of his uncle to try and get some air into his lungs. "Terrible, it was," Grandpa told me, shaking his head.

That's why they all carried gas masks around with them in

the next war. But I thought that was all ancient history. What would Grandpa say about the gassing of Auntie Selma's family?

"The gas bombs fell for three days, thousands more were killed and thousands and thousands wounded," Samir went on. "Naazim says he read about one whole family who all went blind. Aunty Selma lost more than a hundred members of her family."

I can't imagine so many people in one family, and all of them dead. You couldn't fit a hundred people into our little cottage. "That's a very big family," I can't help saying.

"There are a lot of families like that in Iraq," says Samir. "Auntie Selma was only ten. She was sent to live with relatives in Baghdad. She's some sort of distant cousin of my grandfather. She and our uncle Sayeed played together as kids."

"Childhood sweethearts," I say with a bit of a grin.

Samir grins back. "I don't know about that. She says he used to play tricks on her all the time. But then he went away to university and when he came back the family decided they should get married."

That's a bit weird, I think. "Does she love him?" I say cautiously.

"I think so, she misses him a lot. But she also misses all her family. I wasn't born when the Kurds were massacred. Naazim was only a baby. But when he was about fourteen, the year before my father was arrested..."

"When was that?"

"He was taken away in 2002, Naazim turned fourteen in..." He pauses and has a think. "October 2001, so I was eight. Anyway, my father told Naazim what happened to Auntie Selma's family and Naazim told me. I had nightmares for ages."

We are quiet for a minute while I try and take all this in. First of all, Auntie Selma's family are all killed, then when she grows up, she gets married and settles into a new life. Then everything goes wrong again about five years ago. She, Samir and Naazim only just got here alive.

Samir doesn't say anything and I can see he's retreating into being the ice man. I don't blame Samir, I feel the same, all sort of chilly and cold inside. It makes me feel very lost and alone again.

Where's Kim when I need her? I really need to ask her what she thinks about all this stuff. And what about my dad? My biggest problem at the moment is my pathetic parents. Samir hasn't even got any parents. All my problems with Mum and Dad, cleaning the house and keeping the boiler alight, they all seem so silly when I think about everything Auntie Selma and Samir and even Naazim have been through.

I'm fiddling with the green cloth without thinking and suddenly it falls off, revealing a large, heavy-looking book.

Samir leaps to his feet and quickly covers the book again. "You mustn't do that," he says. "It's the Quran. Our Bible."

Everything's so different here what with Auntie Selma's life history on the wall and religious books that have to be covered, let alone a foreign language, which would probably be a lot more interesting to learn than boring old French.

Maybe I'll become fluent in Arabic and become a diplomat in Iraq and help to bring about peace. Then Samir and his family could go home.

Samir says, "I used to bring my father the Quran every morning and he would read to us before breakfast. We had to learn the verses by heart in school, so my father would test us."

He smiles and shakes his head. "Naazim used to call me *ghabi*, stupid, when I made a mistake, and then he'd get told off."

"Do you still read it together?" I ask.

"No..." and his voice fades away. I stare down at the floor and try to think of something to say. Then Samir sighs and says, "We miss my father's voice too much."

We're quiet for a minute, finishing the cola, and it's all so sad that I decide we should talk about something else.

"Did you get into trouble for the exclusion?"

Samir shoots me a little smile of relief and his face clears. Then he says, "I haven't told Auntie Selma or Naazim and school's closed tomorrow for teacher training so I'm hoping they just won't notice."

The door slams downstairs and we both leap to our feet. It's Naazim and suddenly he's in the doorway, the usual glare on his face. Samir doesn't seem to notice and starts chattering away about helping Auntie Selma. But Naazim just keeps glaring at me.

I'm beginning to wonder if I'm wearing the wrong clothes even though I've got my school joggers on and my legs are covered. Not for the first time I wish I'd listened more in Religious Studies lessons. I try to catch Samir's eye but he's just fixed on his big brother.

Then Naazim launches into an interrogation, which makes MI5 look like summer camp, asking me a whole series of questions about brothers and sisters, what my dad does—that one's easy, nothing most of the time—about my mum and even my dog. I'm getting very nervous and flustered when Samir shouts out, "That's enough, Naazim. She's a friend, a good friend."

Naazim stops but you can see he'd rather just juggernaut on and he still hasn't managed to crack a smile. "I'm going to see Auntie Selma," he says, but before he turns to go he says, "Don't speak about the photos."

30. Soaked Again

"Time to go?" I say, and Samir nods.

"Just give me a minute," and he slips out of the room.

I hear him speaking in Arabic. Naazim answers in short grunts and Auntie Selma's laughing. Then he comes back with our jackets and a grin on his face, "Okay, let's go."

What a relief to get outside and away from Naazim's interrogation. I wonder if that's what they taught him in the Iraqi army as we run for the bus. He probably treats every new person like an enemy, automatically. I'd rather pull my eyelashes out than go through that again.

"What's his problem?" I ask once we're on the bus.

"Naazim? He says our parents wouldn't want me to be friendly with a girl, especially if she's not Muslim. It's *haram*, forbidden. Teenagers don't go out with each other in Iraq like they do here. Muslims are very strict," says Samir. "Naazim tries to look after me like Mum and Dad would."

"So that's why he's in a total fury every time he sees me with you," I say.

Samir gives me a shy grin. "He thinks we're going out."

"Oh," I say, and I feel my face go all hot.

We both giggle a little bit and then Samir stares out the

window all the way down the Island while I fiddle about with my cell phone.

It's almost four thirty by the time we're jogging down the road toward the sea, and its beginning to get dark. I can hear the barking of a big dog as we run between the last houses and onto the yacht club road by the inlet. A huge hairy Alsatian, which I think I recognize, is racing over the top of the sand dunes toward the sea. Then with horror I realize it's chasing someone.

It's Mohammed!

He's looking over his shoulder, arms waving about wildly, as he tumbles down the steep slope and onto the beach.

I think my heart's going to stop.

"What's he doing out here?" I yell to Samir as we hurl ourselves over the dunes. Mohammed isn't looking where he's going; he reaches the water's edge and flounders into the sea. At least the water isn't as deep this side of the dunes, unlike on the Solent side where Mohammed was thrown into the sea on Saturday. But it's still very dangerous; you can sink deep into mud on this side of the point.

The dog is barking like mad and Mohammed wades farther and farther and then he trips and falls right in. He splashes like mad and rolls right over onto his back. The dog leaps forward with a delighted bark and plants its huge hairy paws on Mohammed's chest. In horror I see Mohammed's head sink below the surface.

I throw myself down the steep side of the dune and straight into the sea, the freezing water stopping my breath for the second time in less than a week. I hear Samir yelp with the cold as he rushes into the water behind me. My sneakers are sinking into the squelchy mud of the inlet and I'm terrified we'll get stuck and start to sink. But I have to reach Mohammed and get the dog, which I now recognize as Barney, off him.

Where the hell is Mad Murphy, his owner? "Mohammed!" I yell. "Just stay still. He won't hurt you, I promise!"

But Mohammed has stopped splashing and he's almost completely submerged. He can't drown now, he can't!

I lunge forward and grab an arm, hauling him to the surface with all my strength, but I can't do it alone. "Samir, help me!" I shriek, and then he's beside me, grabbing the other arm. I push Barney away with my free hand and he closes his teeth around it, playfully.

"Get off, you stupid mutt," I yell, and he releases my hand after giving it a playful nip.

Mohammed's body feels like a sack of concrete as we start to wade back to the shore. The water is nearly up to my waist and the dog keeps jumping around us, threatening to trip us up.

"Where's his owner?" pants Samir, shifting his grip on our man.

"He doesn't c-c-c-care, he's m-m-mad," I stutter, all my muscles shaking with cold.

This is worse than a full marathon, what with the icy water, the mud sucking at our shoes and the terrible weight of Mohammed. I'm almost at the end of my strength. Suddenly Mohammed's legs give way and he drops down, wrenching my arm almost out of its socket. I lose my grip and both Mohammed and Samir fall forward into the sea. Samir surfaces first, choking and rubbing his eyes. But Mohammed stays under and I'm tearing through the water, grabbing at his arms and shoulders, trying to heave him up.

"We're losing him," I scream as Barney shoves against my legs.

Samir drags himself to his feet, lunges at Mohammed and pulls him upright. Mohammed is gasping and sobbing but we manage to lug him to the shore. We fall onto the beach exhausted. A bitter wind is blowing up from the Solent, chilling me to the bone, and I'm shaking with cold.

Then Mad Murphy appears on top of the dunes and whistles down to Barney. "Not in your way, was he, my lovely boy?" sings out Murphy, and I just glare up at him.

"Won't he tell?" splutters Samir.

I shake my head. "He's bonkers, won't even remember he saw us."

Murphy and Barney wander off along the beach and we start up the dune. But I hear a car approaching slowly from the road. I look over the top of the dune and it's a police car and we're out in the open with Mohammed. The car is crawling along the yacht club road.

"Quick," I hiss to Samir. "Get down into the grass and cover yourselves. I'll try and get rid of them."

Hoping the police won't notice my school trousers are soaked I scramble up onto the concrete road, trying to look as if I'm out for a walk. The car draws up and Good Cop is sitting in the passenger side, the window open.

"Alix, isn't it?" he calls out.

I walk up really close to the car so he can only see my top half and won't notice my knees knocking with terror and cold. "Hi," I say with a cheery smile, "catching some robbers?"

Good Cop gives a hearty laugh and Bad Cop leans over him and snarls, "Seen anyone else down here today?"

"Only Mad Murphy," I say, and we exchange raised eyebrows. No one bothers about him.

"Well, you keep a lookout for anything strange and let us

know, they've just stopped a boat coming around the Isle of Wight with twenty illegal immigrants in it. They'll all go into detention in Portsmouth," says Good Cop.

"Prison?" I ask in a worried voice.

"Just till we can process them and send them back," snarls Bad Cop.

"What if that's too dangerous for them?" I say.

"They get their chance to tell their story," says Good Cop, and they drive off.

I feel as though I'm sweating even though I've probably got hypothermia. I wait until the car is out of sight and then we pull Mohammed to his feet and hurry him away.

Back in the hut I almost yell, "What the hell were you doing? We agreed, Mohammed, you stay in the hut, until...Oh God, do you want us all to go to jail?"

Mohammed can only whisper, "No, no jail, no, please."

"Okay, Alix, he understands," says Samir, on the verge of tears.

Mohammed's face is gray with cold and exhaustion. He doesn't look a lot better than when we pulled him out of the sea on Saturday. He's muttering in Arabic as Samir helps him get into some dry clothes.

It's almost dark now. Samir and me are about to die of cold and I need to bring Mohammed a fresh hot-water bottle and coffee if he's going to survive the night and my clothes are soaking wet and I've lied to the police again.

I can't do this anymore, I think, and feeling completely shattered I slump on the floor, hot tears spurting from my eyes. The police and Dad and Murphy and Barney and the icy water and Mohammed looking as though he's about to die, it's all too much.

Samir is looking at me and he reaches over and shakes my arm a little bit.

"It's okay, Alix, it'll be okay," he keeps saying over and over, and Mohammed keeps muttering in Arabic as though he's lost his mind.

And maybe he has, maybe we all have. I can't even speak. My jaw feels locked in ice. All I can think is, What's Mum going to say when she sees me, and what about Naazim when he sees Samir's wet clothes? Everyone will guess, and then they'll call the police and Bad Cop will get out his handcuffs and Mohammed will get deported...

"What are we going to do?" I sob.

Samir is rubbing my arms frantically, his eyes wide with fear, but I can hardly feel anything. It's getting so dark in this miserable hut but we can't just go home and leave Mohammed.

Then suddenly he calls my name, "Aleex, Aleex."

His gentle voice is shaking with cold but he keeps on saying my name over and over. Then he says, "Go home, Aleex. Go home. You must to go and leave me now. I okay, I okay."

"But you need t-t-to..." I try to speak through my chattering teeth.

"No, go. Go now," he says, and he rolls over in his sleeping bag and mutters something in Arabic to Samir.

"He's right," says Samir in a low voice. "We can't help him if we get sick too. We are his only hope, Alix. We have to leave him now, come back when we are feeling better, at least warmer and dry."

My eyes fill with tears but I know they're right, and then Samir pulls me to my feet and we stumble around to the cottage.

Mum's surprisingly cool and mainly practical about the

whole thing. We tell her we've been mucking about with a bit of wood on the inlet and we fell in.

"I don't know how many times you've come home soaking wet, Alexandra Miller," says Mum sharply. "But it's not clever in this weather, and what about poor Samir? He's not used to our English climate, are you, love?" and Samir gives a shivery shake of his head.

Then she's fussing around on her crutches, flicking on the log-effect gas fire and putting on the kettle. "Go upstairs, you two, and find Samir some of Grandpa's old clothes, and you, young lady, into the bath, while I make the tea," which will be a first since she came out of hospital.

But as I lie in the soothing hot water all I can think of is poor Mohammed and how badly he needs us now. More than ever probably. What on earth was he doing out of the hut on his own? Was he trying to run away, or worse, give himself up?

31. One More Problem

I'm almost dozing off in the bath when I hear a light knocking on the door and Samir's voice calling out, "Alix? You okay?"

"Fine," I say. But actually I feel all hot and bothered with him the other side of the door and me in the bath with nothing on. Did I remember to turn the key?

I get out of the bath and quickly dry myself and put on my nightie and bathrobe.

When I unlock the door Samir's standing there in Grandpa's tatty old trousers and fishing sweater. He's hugging a hot-water bottle Mum must have made for him.

"You look cool," I say, but I feel so weak and tired. I lean against the wall.

Samir grins and says, "Well, I look better than you. The cold really got to you this time. Get into bed with this." He shoves the hot-water bottle into my arms and it feels so good.

Once I'm in bed and Samir's sitting on the end I just don't care about anything anymore. It's pitch-black outside the window and the wind's howling in the tall pines along our road. My bedside clock says 5:57 p.m.

"Why did he leave the hut?" I say in a weak voice. "He's insane."

"He said he felt trapped, like when he was captured and

tortured," says Samir. "He just had to go outside; he only meant to wander about for a few minutes. Then that dog arrived from nowhere and chased him into the water."

"He's crazy, he should've stayed in the hut," I say.

I can't help thinking, If he gets caught, we're all in deep trouble. I can just imagine Bad Cop roaring like an express train in the living room and Good Cop taking out the handcuffs with that smile on his face. He probably has a spare set for Trudy.

"Mohammed said he should have stayed in Iraq, he's sorry he's given us so much trouble," says Samir.

And that's such an awful thought we both fall silent. Samir stands up to leave, clutching a pile of dry clothes for Mohammed, and then he looks down at me and says, "You were so brave going in the sea after Mohammed again. You never stop to think of yourself, you could have drowned, you know."

"So could you," I mutter, embarrassed.

"Well, it's different, I mean Mohammed is my responsibility, I have to save him."

"No way!" I almost yell, only it comes out like a big whisper because I'm so exhausted. "He's *our* responsibility, we're in this together, right?"

Samir's face breaks into the full monty smile.

Then he's gone and even though it's only six o'clock in the evening, I fall into a deep sleep.

I wake up with a jerk. The room is very dark and the wind is wilder than ever around the cottage. The clock says ten past eight and I can hear voices downstairs. A man's voice is speaking quite loudly. It's Dad. Or am I dreaming again? My mouth feels dry from sleep and my legs don't feel as though they have properly woken up.

I go to the top of the stairs and I'm just about to wander

down when I hear Dad say, "You're right, Sheel, I've made a mess of things, but I'll make it up to you, both of you, I promise."

I can't hear everything Mum's saying because she's crying but I hear something about Grandpa, "...didn't even come to my dad's funeral..."

Dad says, "How could I? Gloria had booked Elton John at the Southampton Arena for my birthday. The tickets were a fortune. I couldn't let her down, could I?"

What about letting *us* down? I want to yell out, but then Mum says in a louder voice, "I mean what I say, Johnnie. I'll go to the authorities. Alexandra needs so many things and I've lost my job because of this stupid leg."

I didn't know that! What else are they hiding from me? "All we've got is benefits. You have to pay maintenance for her; I want it every week without fail and you have to see her on Saturdays. She misses you, you stupid idiot."

"I will, I said I will, didn't I? And I mean it this time..."

"You'd better, because God knows what she's up to. What if she gets pregnant with that lad?" Pregnant?!

But I forget the silent button.

Dad comes out into the corridor and sees me at the top of the stairs and says, "You'd better come down."

So I stomp downstairs with my thunderpants face on and yell at Mum, "What do you mean, pregnant...?"

But Mum cuts in, "I don't know where you are half the time or who you're with and you come home soaking wet and you've got that boy with you, Sammy, and you're in the bath and he's upstairs all at the same time. I don't even know his family and..."

"Samir is a friend, that's all," I yell back, even more furious if that's possible, "and he has a very nice auntie and a sort-of-nice

167

brother, well, he's a bit mean, but he's very strict and they're Muslims so they're not allowed girlfriends and anyway I'm too young for sex!"

I swear their jaws drop to their boots.

Even I'm a bit shocked I said that. Imagine if Lindy or the Jayne family heard me. I'd never live it down.

But I'm not in love with anyone right now. Not like Kim and Steven and I don't think they're doing it anyway. "What your mum means, doll," says Dad in a calmer voice, "is that we love you and care about you, and me and your mum…"

"Since when?" I say. "Like, since when is it 'you and Mum'? It's been just me and Mum forever! We have to do everything by ourselves and now I've quit my job so we've got even less money…"

"Quit?" says Mum, eyeing me suspiciously again. "Or did Chaz sack you? What have you done wrong now?"

"He's a racist, if you must know," I yell. "He said he came down here to get away from foreigners in London!"

"He said that?" says Mum, and she's looking quite shocked. "But he always seemed so nice."

"You made the right decision, Alix," says Dad firmly. "We don't do racism."

Well, he passed that test at least, I think with relief. "You've got to concentrate on your schoolwork and go to college and not worry about money anymore. That's our job, right, Sheel?"

And Mum sighs and leans back in her armchair and says quietly, "You'd better stick to it, Johnnie, or you know what I'll do."

And I know it sounds like blackmail, but she doesn't really have a choice, does she?

Dad gets up and zips his jacket and I walk to the front door with him. He puts his arms tight around me and it feels so good to be hugged by someone who is stronger than me for once.

"How's about you and me mosey on down to the li'l ol' bowling alley Saturday morning, doll?" he says in American, and I can't help giving a bit of a smile.

"Wearing my pants?" I drawl back.

"Heck yeah! Nine sharp and don't you give me no excuses." He thrusts something into my hand and he's gone. When I open my fingers I see it's a twenty-pound note. Wow!

"Alix?" says Mum, and she's not even using the full name. I go back into the living room and she's close to tears again. "It's okay, Mum, honest," I say, feeling quite worried. Should I call the doctor?

But Mum says, "Your Dad and I have made such a mess of things. You've been doing everything for me and all I do is snap at you, but it's because..." And she stops and gives me such a sad look. But then she goes on, "Your dad thought it was best to make a clean break when he went. He thought it would be easier for you. Anyway, the Gremlin doesn't like kids," and her tone is really nasty.

"And you didn't want me to see him either, be honest," I say with a frown.

"Can you blame me, the way he walked out on me? I was furious, I didn't see why he should have you and not me."

She sounds so whiny I feel the anger welling up inside me again. Why should I be punished because Mum and Dad can't sort out their problems? But I manage to keep quiet. It's just not worth it sometimes, is it?

Mum's still going on, "And then your grandpa died and I think I got, you know, a bit miserable with everything..." A *bit* miserable.

"Breaking my leg was the last straw. I just gave up, I suppose. Neither of us were thinking about you. I'm so sorry, darling, I've been so selfish."

That does it. I'm nearly crying now and I go over and put my arms around her and we sit like that for a few minutes, sniffing into each other's sweaters, and then I say, "Shall I make us a cup of tea?"

We stay up until late watching a James Bond movie and making popcorn in the microwave and it's the best evening we've had since Grandpa died.

Only there's still Mohammed to sort out, isn't there?

32. Betrayed

Mum wants me to stay home today. She knows that school's closed for teacher training.

"We could have a nice quiet day together, order a takeout for lunch."

"I can't," I say, trying not to notice the disappointment in her face. "I'm meeting up with Kim and Samir in the library. We've got course work to do and I need some of their notes."

"They could come here," says Mum, brightening up at the thought. "We've got plenty of food for lunch."

But I can't, can I? Just as things sort out at home it's all kicking up outside. I can't remember the last time I had an ordinary day, washing my hair and downloading music onto my MP3 player. It's only been five days since we hid Mohammed but it feels more like five years. How much longer can we keep our big secret?

Steven has arranged a meeting at the burger bar in town with some refugee rights group, and Samir wants me there so that we can decide if it's safe to take them to meet Mohammed.

We can't fail him now, can we?

So I take a leaf out of Mum's book and say, "I've gotten behind, what with the broken leg and everything. We've got exams at the end of term and I've got to get good marks. Kim and Samir are going to help me catch up."

Well, if she can blackmail Dad then I can tell a lie. It's all for a good cause, isn't it? So Mum finally agrees to let me go and then I have to squeeze out the door without Trudy, who's jumping up at me in a total canine frenzy. "I'll make it up to you, my angel, I promise," I cry out as I pull the front door shut.

My phone rings as I wait for the bus. It's Kim. "It's my turn next," she breathes.

Oh my God, her clarinet audition, I'd forgotten, what kind of a best friend am I? "You'll be fine, deep breaths. I'll see you at the burger bar."

"Okay," and she clicks off.

As the bus rolls forward over Langstone Bridge the water is flat calm after last night's storm. Just like before a tsunami. Grandpa said you only know the big wave is coming if all the water sucks out from the beach way out to sea. That's the warning it's building up to a humongous wave, which will cover everything. It feels like our storm is gathering, with the police nosing around and Lindy at the hideout and Terrence down on the Island. If the refugee people can't save Mohammed, then we could be completely engulfed.

If I'm honest, it isn't my life I'm worried about. The ones who would really have to ride out the big wave would be Mohammed. And Samir, Naazim and Auntie Selma.

What could Kim or me or Steven do to save them? They might go to prison here or they might even be deported back to Iraq to torture, prison or even death.

As we pull up to the bus stop I see Liam, Lindy's boyfriend, wander past with his long, greasy hair falling over his face. But no sign of Lindy. I'm pretty certain she's just playing a game with us. Eventually she'll give us away either to Terrence or the police. When it suits her. She's probably told Liam all about it by now as well.

Time's running out. So many people are either in on this or beginning to put two and two together. How long before someone gives us away to the police?

And what about Mrs. Saddler? She's nosing around more and more, turning up at the cottage and winding Mum up about where I am and what I'm up to. Not surprising really as she's always charging around the beaches with Jeremy, who can hardly keep up with her on his dinky dachshund legs. I'm amazed she hasn't turned up at the hut, booming at Mohammed to get dressed and get out of here, smartish young man!

I have to clear my head so I sprint to the burger bar. Steven and Kim are already there when I arrive panting—I'm so out of condition—and they're holding hands under the table. Kim's face is quite flushed but that could just be from the pressure of the audition.

As soon as I sit down she launches into this massive and detailed description, "...I just managed to do the chromatics when my reed split and I had to change it and my hands were trembling so much I dropped the reed packet and that cow of a conductor tutted! Can you believe that? Actually tutted at me! I nearly died. How mean can you get?"

All I can do is nod and smile and try to follow, not having a clue what chromatics or any of this stuff means. Even Steven's eyes are beginning to glaze over and he decides to get the cappuccinos. That gives me a chance to leap on Kim.

"So come on, spill," I interrupt before she launches into a full-blown description of the life of Mozart. "You and Steven, getting quite close?"

That stops her. Kim looks at me with her hazel-green eyes, unblinking, and then she says in this breathy voice, "He's amazing. He gave me this for luck today." She pulls out a silver chain with a locket from under her sweater. "Look inside," and she opens it. There's a tiny bar of black music notes drawn beautifully on a piece of creamy card.

"Wow," I say. Will anyone ever love me, I think, with a pang of jealousy? But when do I have time for love right now?

Steven comes back with the coffees. He sits down and looks impatiently at his watch. "They should have been here twenty minutes ago."

"Which group did you get hold of?" I mumble through a mouthful of foam.

"RROK, RefugeeRightsOK. They've said they can help Mohammed to get justice and hopefully the right to stay in Britain. They have lawyers who specialize in refugees. I spent ages on the phone to them yesterday. Mum reckons they're the best on the south coast. I told her it was research for Citizenship."

"Good one." I nod and then I see Lindy outside in the square and coming toward her, spread out in a line, are Terrence and two of his gang, including blond Gaz from the beach. Now what?

Lindy shoots a glance across at us and there's something in her look that makes me put my cup down. She nods toward the far corner of the square and to my horror I see Samir. His head is down and his hood up so he hasn't noticed the gang. Yet.

"Come on," I say, springing to my feet.

"No, Ali," says Kim, grabbing my arm. "It's not safe."

But I shrug her off. "I'm not leaving Samir on his own with Terrence ever again."

But really I'm terrified and I'm secretly hoping Liam will

turn up. I mean, he's twenty, so much older than Terrence, surely he'd get rid of him and his gang.

But as I go outside the burger bar there's no sign of Liam, just Terrence and that horrible Gaz and another smaller boy who looks just as mean. Samir has reached me now and I hear Steven and Kim coming up behind. Lindy has stopped and because it's only midmorning on a Wednesday there's hardly anyone else around.

"Oy! Paki!" yells out Terrence, and we freeze. "Got ya now, ain't we!" What does he mean?

"Tell him what ya done, mate." Gaz laughs and he sounds so evil.

"Phoned the police about your Taliban friend. Didn't ya hear the sirens? They'll rip that hut apart and chuck him back in the sea!" roars Terrence.

The whole gang starts to laugh and push each other around and jump up and down with their arms hanging low, like apes.

I can't believe it! They've given Mohammed away, betrayed him to the police, and that means we're all in deep trouble.

But there's no time to think straight because Samir sweeps the hood from his head and screams at Terrence, "You bastard, I'll kill you!" and before I can do anything he launches himself at Terrence, fist and feet flying and they both tip over to the ground. For a few seconds Terrence is under Samir and I even think that Samir is going to win. And then there is a terrible groan. Just that. One big groan.

Samir goes limp and Terrence swats him away like a fly and yells to his gang, "Run!"

The gang are gone in a second. There's blood everywhere. All over Samir's hands and sweatshirt and the pavement.

His face is white as sea mist, his eyes shut. He's dead, I think, numbly. Like all the people on Auntie Selma's wall.

No, he can't be!

The blood is making me feel sick just like back at the hut, and my mind whirls with images and words all jumbling up together.

Already people are gathering and I can hear sirens blaring. Tears are pouring down my face and I'm whispering, "Don't die, don't die."

Then Samir's eyes flicker open and I cry out in relief. His lips move slowly and then he croaks, "Go to the hut. Save him." And his eyes close again.

"He's alive! Where's the ambulance?" I yell to Kim.

But Kim is speaking to me and she's telling me to go to Mohammed. I can't take it in at first but she keeps saying over and over in a low voice, "I'll stay with Samir, don't worry, Ali, you must go."

And I know she's right. Then I'm running toward the bus station. I can hear someone running behind me but I don't look back. In my pocket is Dad's twenty-pound note. There's no time for a bus and I see a minicab, wrench open the door and yell, "Sandy Point, as quick as you can!"

But as I throw myself into the backseat the other door opens and someone else gets in.

It's Lindy!

33. Tracked Down

The taxi pulls away at a cruising speed. I want it to go faster but the driver won't break the speed limit, even though I tell him it's an emergency.

"Ring the police then, love," he says. Well, I'm hardly likely to do that, am I?

I turn on Lindy, "What're you doing in my taxi? Why did you tell your disgusting brother about the hut?"

Lindy shrugs and stares out the window. I grab her shoulder and wrench her around. "What's your game, you cow?"

Lindy eyes me as if I'm some sort of slug and then she says, "What if Terrence follows you? What'll you do then?" That makes me go cold. She's right. I can't face Terrence on my own. But it still doesn't add up. "How does he know about Mohammed anyway, you must have told him."

Lindy's staring out of window again and she says in her bored voice, "He guessed, I didn't say nothing."

"Liar," I yell, and I feel like smacking her one. "How could he guess where the hideout was?"

The driver is getting fed up with us and he snaps over his shoulder, "Settle down, girls, I don't want any trouble, and which one of you is going to pay for this?"

I show him the twenty-pound note and he relaxes. At least Dad's good for something for once, I think.

"Terrence guessed the same way I did, saw you running in and out of the bushes. You bunch of losers," says Lindy. "No idea how to keep a secret."

You can imagine the secrets they keep in her family. We're on the last mile before the yacht club road and it feels as if we're moving in slow motion. We must get there before the police and smuggle Mohammed away to my house. Mum will have to cooperate or I'll threaten to run away from home. This is desperate.

Then Lindy says, "Is Two Percent dead?"

"What do you care?" I snarl back and she gives a slight shrug but she doesn't look away.

"I don't know," I say grudgingly, "but he spoke to me before I left."

She gives a brief nod and not for the first time I wonder if she really is as bad as the rest of her family. After all, she could have given Mohammed away herself and instead she helped him with his wounds. But I still don't trust her.

We finally get to the top of the yacht club road and the driver refuses to go any farther. "Private road, I'll get a ticket," he complains, but I think he's just lazy.

I pay him and leap out of the car and start running. I can feel panic rising up inside me and then Grandpa's voice sounds in my head. "When you're out at sea," he used to say when we were standing on the beach and watching all the boats tack from side to side, "keep your rudder steady, don't sail too close to the wind, too risky."

Just having Lindy here feels like taking a huge risk, but it's too late now.

I slow my breathing as I run to calm myself, like my marathon trainer taught us. At least I don't have to get into the news-papers to get Dad's attention. Don't need to now if he keeps his promise. That would be a first.

I can hear Lindy puffing away behind me trying to keep up. Then I'm crawling through the hole in the fence and she's close behind me, complaining about snagging her tights on the wire. I scramble through the bushes panting hard, terrified what I will find. But the padlock is still gleaming on the locked door.

When we get around the side Lindy says, "I'll stay here, keep an eye out for Terrence."

I hesitate for a nanosecond and then throw myself through the window, calling out, "Mohammed, get up, grab your stuff!"

But Mohammed is slumped in the sleeping bag and I have to shake him awake. "The police are coming."

That does it. His eyes open and fear floods his face. He starts muttering in Arabic and fumbling with the zip.

I grab a plastic bag and start filling it. The bag splits almost immediately and everything spills back onto the floor. Moham-med climbs slowly out of his sleeping bag and starts pulling on his shoes.

"Use the sleeping bag, you muppet," sneers Lindy through the window. Of course, that's what I did the first time! Very quickly I've packed up everything and emptied the hut, leaving just a patch on the floor where some juice spilt.

I bundle Mohammed out the window and throw the sleep-ing bag onto the ground. Outside Mohammed leans up against the hut wall, his eyes closed, breathing heavily. How far can he get like this? And then I hear the sirens.

Lindy and I lock eyes and for a second she looks as scared as me.

Did I misjudge her too?

"We have to get out of sight," I hiss.

I grab Mohammed with one arm and stagger off toward the bushes, practically dragging him along. Lindy tags behind, dragging the sleeping bag along the ground.

The sirens have stopped and I can hear men's voices near the Lifeboat Station, shouting, "Over here, must be that old hut."

Did Terrence give them the GPS coordinates as well?

We stumble toward the bushes and I'm nearly in tears. Mohammed falls down twice and Lindy drags the sleeping bag while I pick him up. I'm waiting for her to yell to the cops, "This way!" but she doesn't say anything.

We finally reach the bushes beyond the hut. They are really dense and for the first time since Samir was stabbed I feel a flicker of hope. We'll burrow deep inside the thicket, wait for the police to give up and leave. Then we'll go back to my house and...

But my imagination fails me as Mohammed's legs give way and he falls so heavily against me I tip backward and crack my head on the ground. I can almost feel my brains rattle and I lie there with my eyes closed for what seems like ages.

When I open my eyes again the sky spins above me and there is a sharp pain in the back of my head. Mohammed is sprawled across my body and I can hardly breathe. Freezing water from a puddle is soaking my hair and I'm thinking, It's over, give it up while you can.

But Mohammed is groaning and he needs me more than ever. So still feeling really groggy I manage to push him off and get up on my knees.

Lindy is standing over us, staring down.

"Pick up the bag," I snap, "and get it in the bushes." She gives me a surprised look and then just does it silently.

I grab Mohammed's face with both hands and whisper, "Come on, nearly there," but he doesn't move. There's nothing for it, I have to pull him myself. I grab him by the feet and heave and heave until I think my shoulders will dislocate. I can only move him a few yards at a time.

We're not going to make it, I think in a panic, as the voices of the police come closer and closer.

But I finally get him under the bushes and out of sight. Just in time!

Squinting through the leaves, I can see two policemen come around the corner of the hut and lean into the open window.

It's Good Cop and Bad Cop.

If Lindy even looks as though she's going to call out I'll throw myself on her and throttle her.

But instead of Lindy giving us away there is a terrifying rustle in the bushes behind us.

Oh my God! We've been discovered!

34. Enemy or Friend?

"I came as soon as I could. The bus went so slowly." It's Trumpet Steven and he's whispering in my ear.

He spots Mohammed lying in a heap on the ground and in a louder voice he says, "Oh God, he's dead."

I slap a hand over his mouth and pull him down. "No, he's not," I hiss.

When I let him go he whispers back, "What are we going to do now?"

I've never heard him sound so uncertain. His voice has lost that cool, grown-up tone and he looks a real mess, twigs in his hair, mud smeared all down his jacket.

Then he catches sight of Lindy crouching under a bush. "What are *you* doing here?" he hisses at her.

Lindy snorts and says, "She'd never manage by herself, would she?" She nods toward me and, of course, she's right. "Anyhow, I'm sick of Terrence, he bullies me all the time."

Well, that makes sense. Terrence bullies everyone, it's hardly surprising he started at home.

Then I hear Bad Cop roar out in his gunshot voice, "Nothing here, better search the area."

They're coming!

Has it all been for nothing, the lies and the hiding?

Maybe Mum and Dad are right and this is what it means to run wild, even though I'm not pregnant or on drugs.

But if I can't keep Mohammed safe now, then Samir will never forgive me. Those pleading eyes will turn to defeat and he'll never trust anyone again. Samir will stay an ice man for the rest of his life.

"Alix, quick, what shall we do?" hisses Steven, his face tense with fear.

I'm beginning to realize that brains plus trumpet playing don't necessarily equal common sense.

I glance at my watch and make an instant decision.

"Get Mohammed up to the road. The bus is due in two minutes. Just get him on the bus and out of here. Ring your friends from that refugee group and tell them to hide him away until the search dies down."

Steven is staring at me, his face pale. He's probably wondering what his mum will say. I give him a push and hiss, "Go on! I'll stall the police while you get away."

I stand up and start pushing through the bushes. Lindy's so close behind me I can feel her breath on my neck. Mohammed grunts as Steven heaves him to his feet and I turn to look but they've already gone, taking the sleeping bag with them.

We're out in the open now and I'm covered in prickles and leaves, my sneakers black with mud.

Good Cop spots us first. "Hey, you kids, what are you doing here?" he calls out.

This is it, I think. I have to stall them, think up excuses, give Steven time to get to the bus and away. But my throat has closed up and my brain scrambles terrifying images of Mohammed. He could be on a plane back to Iraq before dark and beheaded tomorrow morning!

I can't bear to think of Samir's horrified face, while Naazim rattles on like a road drill about what we've been doing. If they go to prison, will I be allowed to visit them?

Then Bad Cop says, "Aren't you Terrence Bellows's sister?" and points his truncheon, which is fully open, straight toward Lindy.

I couldn't be caught with anyone worse. What if she tells them everything now? Then of course she'll go laughing to her stinking brother about how dumb I look in handcuffs. This is probably what she's been planning all along. Why did I ever think I could trust her? Oh God.

Bad Cop is still speaking, "Right, you," and he's pointing at me now. "You live down here. Someone's been camping out in this hut. What have you seen? I want the truth, now," and he's waving the truncheon at both of us.

Tell them the truth? What is the truth? That we've saved someone from drowning and now they need to ask the queen for asylum? I can't see them being very happy about that.

"We got a phone call from your brother, the one who's not in jail yet," sneers Good Cop rounding on Lindy. "Something about an illegal hiding out here. And now you two show up. Where is he? In the bushes?" and he starts to push past us.

Lindy opens her mouth to speak and I wait for all hell to break loose. "You're nuts," she says in a bored voice. "My brother's a psycho."

The cops stop and stare at her.

She's just trying to save her skin and Terrence's, I'm raging to myself.

"What do you mean, young lady?" says Good Cop.

"Don't you play games with us, we haven't got time," cuts in

Bad Cop in his best rottweiler voice. I can almost feel his jaws closing around my throat.

"It was probably a hoax call, you dumbos," she says.

She's almost laughing in their faces. My head spins around again. Aren't they going to arrest her for being cheeky?

But Lindy hasn't finished. "He's always doing it." She's really enjoying herself as the cops glare at her.

"We don't know nothing about illegal people do we, Ali?" And she looks at me, her head tipped, eyebrows raised.

We? Is she kidding? Me and Lindy Bellows, mates? I rub my aching head and for a second I think I'm in a coma and I'm dreaming all this.

Then Lindy raises her eyebrows slowly and her eyes are boring into mine as if to say, Just play along, can't you?

I stare back and then I slowly shake my head.

The cops exchange exasperated looks and Good Cop snaps, "So what are you doing here?"

"Hanging out," says Lindy as if that's nothing unusual. "We always hang out and go for walks on the beach, don't we, Ali?"

All I can do is nod.

Bad Cop opens his mouth, a nasty look on his face, and then a voice crackles over his walkie-talkie. He moves away from us and booms out, "Yes, what? Yes, yes, okay, we'll take it now." Then he turns to Good Cop and snarls, "You won't believe this. Terrence Bellows has stabbed a boy in town. He's been spotted heading down the Island. We have to get after him."

Good Cop nods and says to us, "We'll be around to speak to you girls later with your parents," and they make off through the bushes back to the road.

I'm left alone with my new best friend, Lindy Bellows.

35. Mermaids

"I'm off," says Lindy, and she's gone before I get a chance to say...Well, what could I say? Thank you? How come we're best friends suddenly? Kim's never going to believe what just happened.

Then my phone bleeps. It's a message from Kim, she must be psychic. *S in hsptal. Nt srious. Seen Steven?*

I almost go weak with relief. Samir is safe and I let out a bit of a whoop. I text her back to meet Steven off the bus with Mohammed. Then I scramble back through the bushes, out of the Nature Reserve and around the back of the Lifeboat Station, scanning the beaches.

I can't see anyone except Barney and Mad Murphy running over the beach. They almost look like a pair of dolphins rising and falling with the swell out at sea.

My head still feels very sore as I stumble back home. There's no sign of the bus or the police. With any luck Steven and Mohammed will be in town in about twenty minutes while the cops are distracted chasing Terrence Bellows around the Island.

The next bus isn't due for an hour. I need to go home and get some cash. I didn't wait for change from the taxi driver, which was stupid. I'm just wondering how much money I've got, less than a pound I think, when my phone goes.

It's Mum. She absolutely never rings my cell phone except in a dire emergency and the last time was when Grandpa died and all she did was ask me to come home really quickly. Why is she ringing me now? Maybe she's had another fall and she can't get up. I press the answer button.

"Alix, darling, where are you? Are you in town? You must come home immediately, or no, perhaps it's better to go home with Kim, stay together whatever you do and I'll get Kevin to bring you home..."

"Whoa, slow down, Mum. What's up?" I say, but I think I can guess.

"There's been a stabbing in town. Some sort of gang trouble. I thought that only went on in London. Anyway, Mrs. Saddler's here, she heard it from Bert's divorced son. His friend rang..."

"Okay, okay, don't worry. I'll be home in about one minute."

I walk slowly to give myself time to think. The neighbors must have seen all the activity around here this morning. They don't miss much. God knows how much longer we could have kept everything secret from them anyhow. Mrs. Saddler was already getting suspicious, wasn't she?

Both Mum and Trudy fall on me when I get in the house. I don't know who needs me more! Trudy is desperate for a wee so I let her out in the back garden. Mum's totally emotional, blubbering all over her crutches as she stomps around after me.

"Thank God you're home, you must have missed the gang, oh, Alix darling, I was so scared. What a day to shut the school. If you were all in class this would never have happened," Mum rattles on.

I decide to keep quiet, the less I say the better. But the doorbell goes and would you believe it's Mad Murphy with Barney.

Mum has a soft spot for Murphy so she calls him in and it's weird to see him in our hallway, looming over us like some sort of benevolent scarecrow.

"Make everyone a pot of tea, Alix," says Mum.

Everyone? I put my head around the living room door and I swear half the street are there. What do they think this is? New Year's Eve? Mrs. Saddler is sitting in the best armchair and Bert and his divorced son and the neighbor from the other side, with the twins, are all crammed on the sofa, and Barney is already sniffing around. Trudy's come back in and she starts wuffing at him to play all over our tiny living room.

I come back a few minutes later with the tea tray and they're all talking at once. "The police came and asked me if I'd seen any unusual boats dropping illegal immigrants, like, around Sandy Point," Bert's saying in his slow, ponderous voice. "We would have noticed that, wouldn't we, lad?" and his son nods his head.

"Have you seen anything?" the twins' mum asks Mrs. Saddler.

"Nothing," says Mrs. Saddler, shaking her head firmly. But she's eyeing me closely and I feel as though she can see right into my brain.

"Illegal immigrants on Hayling Island, how daft is that," says Bert scornfully.

"No, it isn't." And everyone stops dead and looks at Mad Murphy. "Barney and me see all sorts no one else sees."

I'm holding my breath as he pauses, and he's looking at me in a really strange way. The room's gone silent and I think, When he gives me away shall I run? Or just sit here until the police come?

"Like what, Murphy, love?" says Mum softly. I've practically died from lack of air.

Then Murphy gives Mum a huge smile and says, "A mermaid, Sheila. Coming out of the sea, with beautiful black hair. You've seen one, Alix, haven't you?"

Everyone looks at me curiously and for a second I don't know what to do. And then I say, "Sure, Murphy, I've seen loads of them carrying seashells and stuff."

That does it. They all start laughing and saying stuff like, "Pass the sugar before the mermaid takes it all," and "Does she have a sister, maybe your son could ask her out, Bert" and Bert laughs his sort of hyena-choking laugh while his son sits there with his usual blank look on his face.

Murphy has morphed back into the village idiot and he practically swipes Mrs. Saddler's teacup from her, so Mum gently eases him out the door. I'm just about to escape to my bedroom and ring Kim to find out if Steven and Mohammed have arrived in town when the doorbell goes again. It's Chaz. I can't believe it.

"Alix," he cries out as if we're old friends. In your dreams, I think.

"I heard everyone was here," he says in an excited voice. Typical, I think, news travels so fast on the Island. "You'll never believe what's happened," and he pushes past me into the living room.

Mum's face goes quite dark when she sees him but Chaz doesn't seem to notice. "Have you heard about all them illegal immigrants?" he says to everyone. "Hiding out somewhere near the beach. You can't trust them, you know, that's why I moved down here."

Trust Chaz to get his facts wrong. Just like the rubbish newspapers he reads. But what about the neighbors? What do they think? I look around the room at the people I have grown up with on Hayling Island and I think of all the times I could have asked them what they believed in and how I had never bothered. Well, I'm going to find out now, aren't I?

Everyone shifts uncomfortably. It's Mrs. Saddler who speaks out first in her booming voice, "What do you mean, 'them'?"

"You know, asylum seekers and immigrants and all that. Come to take our benefits, that's all they're here for."

Bert says, "Well, you can't lump people together like that, right, lad? Got to give people a chance, like. Can't just assume all foreigners are up to no good. Some people come from terrible places, right, lad?"

"Right, Dad," says his son in a really loud voice.

There's a bit of a silence and then I say nervously, "Everyone's allowed to ask for asylum, we did it in school." Chaz's eyebrows shoot upward until they look like they're going to fly off his face but a wave of shuffling and mutters of agreement wash around the room.

Yess! I think in relief and almost yell it out loud.

"Well, it's all right down here," says Chaz, "that's why I love it here. But it ain't like this in London, it's like there's no one white left..."

"Color's only skin deep," booms Mrs. Saddler, cutting Chaz off.

The twins' mother mutters in agreement. "Bert's right, you have to give people a chance."

Bert beams and his son gives him a nod.

"We Islanders have always welcomed visitors," Mrs. Saddler points out proudly. "Just like you, Chaz. We made you welcome, didn't we?"

"Oh, I give them all a chance, me," says Chaz quickly, and he's looking a bit embarrassed. After all, these are all his customers. "I serve anyone in my shop, you tell them, Alix." He turns around and fixes his eyes on me.

I feel myself go all red and hot. I don't know what to say to that but Chaz doesn't wait for an answer. He steams on, "I ain't racist, me, just want to live among me own kind for a change."

There's a general muttering around the room and then Mum says, "We all know how hard you've worked in the business since you took over." Here we go, I think, she's giving in to him. "But," she goes on, "I think everyone here agrees with Mrs. Saddler that Hayling Island has always welcomed visitors. We expect you to do the same."

Way to go, Mom! I think in American.

Chaz stands there for a moment and I can almost hear him thinking and then he says, "Fair enough."

"Good," says Mrs. Saddler in a tone that makes it clear that his views are not shared by the other people here.

Chaz rattles his keys in his pocket and shuffles his feet. Then he says, "Well, got customers waiting," and I see him to the door.

As he starts down the path he hesitates and turns back to me. "Your job's still open, Alix," he says, and his eyes are sort of puzzled looking.

I think for a few seconds and then I say, "Okay, I'll give it another go."

His face relaxes into a slight smile and says, "Good, see yer in the morning, seven sharp?"

I nod and he goes off.

When I go back in the living room everyone's talking at once. I'm really anxious to find out how Samir is. How much longer are they all going to stay? Mum's even muttering about making another pot of tea!

"What did Chaz want?" she asks me.

"Oh, just to make sure I wasn't late for my paper route tomorrow," I say, holding open the living room door as a sort of hint to the neighbors.

Mum stares at me for a minute and then she says, "Hmm, well, see how it goes."

She turns to Mrs. Saddler and says, "Did you know, Margaret, that Alix has been watching all about refugees on the news? She keeps asking such interesting questions."

"I've always said she's a clever girl," says Mrs. Saddler with a smug grin.

Has she? That's news to me.

Finally everyone starts to leave, piling their cups onto the tea tray and saying loud good-byes and to look out for mermaids, until it's only Mum, me and Mrs. Saddler left.

"My Jeremy is very good at sniffing out anything strange," says Mrs. Saddler mysteriously.

Then she says to Mum, "She's a good girl, your Alix. Knows right from wrong. You've done a good job, Sheila Miller, and no husband to help you."

Mum goes a bit red and I bend down to give Trudy a good cuddle so that they can't see me looking embarrassed.

As I watch Mrs. Saddler go down the path, I think, You should never judge someone until you get to know them. Everyone deserves a chance. Even Lindy, I decide grudgingly.

Then Mum says, "Alexandra," and I'm about to say, It's Alix with an i, when she grins and says, "How about takeout?"

And then I tell her it was Samir who was stabbed.

36. Safe House

Mum is really shaken about Samir and she starts on about how dangerous it is in town now. "You'll have to stay at home until the police catch the gang. I don't want Terrence Bellows coming after you," she says.

Is she mad? "I have to see Samir," I say, pulling on my jacket and grabbing my keys. Trudy is whimpering up at me and Mum's eyes are filling with frightened tears. "I have to make sure he's all right, Mum, don't you understand?"

"Alix, please..." But I'm already out the door.

It's hard to leave her like that but I have to see for myself, make sure Samir is alive. There was so much blood.

And I'm also worried about whether Steven managed to get Mohammed safely away. This is such a mess and there is so much to sort out.

As I sprint down the path she yells out, "I'm calling your father," but I just keep going.

A bus pulls up just as I get to the corner. I leap on, run upstairs and call Kim. "Where are you, how's Samir?"

"I've just left the hospital," she says. "They won't let me see him. His auntie's here and his brother. Not very smiley, is he?"

"Didn't they tell you anything? Has Samir had stitches, what about his insides, they must be all messed up?"

"I don't know anything, Ali, but one of the nurses followed me out and said not to worry too much."

"I suppose that's good, isn't it?" But I wasn't sure. What if his organs are sliced up, like his liver. Do you die if you get stabbed in the liver? I even think about calling Lindy with her first aid training, but I don't know her number.

"I finally got hold of Steven, he's gone with you-know-who somewhere safe," says Kim in a whisper. "I'll meet you off the bus."

It's a bit Lara Croft, all this secrecy, but actually, right now all I want is to make sure everyone's safe and no one's mortally injured. Not asking much, am I?

The bus is held up by traffic and I seriously consider jumping off and running all the way into town. Then we're crossing Langstone Bridge. The tide is going out and I can see the remains of the old Wadeway stretching out in a long green line. The Wadeway goes back more than a thousand years. Before there was a bridge it was the only way to reach Hayling Island at low tide. I've tried walking on it but it's very slippery with seaweed. If you fall off into the mud you can sink up to your neck in places. The coast guard has to rescue people every year.

Rescue. That's all I seem to think about these days. So many people in my life need to be rescued.

Like my mum, who can hardly walk, has lost her job and now she's applying for benefits. So why didn't she tell me that?

My dad's such a loser so even if we are going to start meeting up again—and I'm really glad we are because I didn't realize how much I missed him until I saw him again—it's a good thing I decided to give the paper route another go. With parents like mine I need to earn money so that I can rescue them.

Mohammed and Steven will need rescuing if the police catch up with them.

And what about Lindy? It looks like she needs rescuing from her brother, probably her entire family. She could have given us away but she didn't.

No one's going to rescue me. Not since Grandpa died.

As the bus pulls into town Mum's words ring through my head, "What if Terrence comes after you?" I can't help looking around nervously but there's no sign of anyone from the Bellows family.

Kim almost drags me off the bus and starts pulling me down the road, speaking in a rapid, low voice. "Mohammed's in a house near school."

"Is it safe?" I mutter back as we hurry along. My heart is thumping in my chest and all I can think is, We have to get there before the police. How many more chances will we have before he's caught? Before we're all caught? A chill scutters down my spine.

Kim goes into a street I don't know and knocks on the door of a middle terrace house.

The door opens a crack, a young man peers out at us and then says, "Come in."

We go inside a narrow hall and a man with long blond hair tied back in a ponytail leads the way into the kitchen at the back.

"Mohammed!" I cry out, and there he is, sitting on a chair. I've never seen him on a chair before. He looks totally different, sort of normal, ordinary.

"Aleex, my friend," he says, and tries to stand up but another guy who looks Indian, with short black hair, in jeans and a T-shirt, stops him.

"You need to rest, Mohammed, Alix understands, okay?" He looks at me and I nod.

"Pritesh," he says, offering his hand and we shake. It feels very grown-up. "This is Jerry, we're from RROK, RefugeeRightsOK. Your friend Steven contacted us and told us all about Mohammed and how you've been hiding him. That's so amazing."

Kim gives me a grin and I can't help feeling a bit pleased. Mohammed is nodding and looking at me with his sad dark eyes and they remind me so much of Samir's eyes when he was lying bleeding on the square, begging me to get to the hut before the police, that I feel tears welling up. Should I have gone to the hospital first? But Samir will want to know what's happened to Mohammed.

Steven comes in and he and Kim hug each other as if they haven't met for months. Everyone laughs and I feel a bit better. So I say, "What can you do for Mohammed?"

"A human rights lawyer will come and meet him here tomorrow," says Pritesh. "He'll help Mohammed to put in an application for asylum through the proper channels."

"What channels? How do you know that's safe? They could send him straight back to Iraq."

These two don't look much older than me. What do they really know? Samir would never forgive me if I make a mistake now after everything we've been through.

Then Mohammed says, "I know you are scared, Aleex," his voice calms me a little, it feels almost familiar now, "but you don't have to worry no more. You are brave, you take me from the freezing English seas. I am dying from drowning and cold and afraid of being..."

"...beheaded." It just slips out and Kim gives a gasp. The room goes very quiet and Pritesh and Jerry exchange looks.

They're probably deciding to send us home and I don't know what I'll tell Samir. Should I take Mohammed back to the hut?

Then Jerry says, "RROK is campaigning to change the law so that people like Mohammed who were interpreters for the British army in Iraq, even for a few months, are allowed to stay here. We're very hopeful. It's obvious that Mohammed has been tortured and that it would be very dangerous to deport him."

That sounds a bit better. I look straight at Mohammed and say, "I don't know if Samir would agree."

Mohammed reaches for a bottle of mineral water on the table and takes a sip. His movements are slow and deliberate. I can see he's in a lot of pain but he's looking very thoughtful.

Then he says, "You must to decide for him."

Everyone is looking at me—so no change there—and I feel as if I'm weighed down with a great bag of Hayling breakwater stones that even an elephant couldn't move. I have to make the biggest decision of my life and it's for someone else. For Samir. If he feels I've let him down then he'll stay an ice man forever and never trust anyone again. What would he want me to do?

Then I remember his words on the beach, when he was talking about the river that runs through Baghdad and playing with his friend Daoud. Samir said he couldn't be deported now because he has proper permission to stay.

"Samir wants Mohammed to have refugee status like him and Naazim and Auntie Selma. Then he can't be deported and he can stay here and work or go to university. "

Pritesh is listening to me very seriously. Perhaps I judged him and Jerry too quickly. I thought I'd stopped doing that.

"We have a lot of experience with gaining refugee status for asylum seekers," Pritesh says, and he does sound as if he knows what he's talking about. "It'll be obvious to anyone that Mohammed needs safe asylum in England. We're very confident with our lawyers." He glances at Jerry who gives a firm nod.

That's what Samir wants, isn't it?

I take a deep breath and say, "Okay."

37. Gremlins

Why isn't it the weekend yet? I don't want to go to school, but it's only Thursday. I'm sure Spicer will make me do the detention I skipped and that means I won't be able to go and see Samir straight after school. I'm desperate to tell him all about Mohammed and RROK and the lawyer, but it'll be difficult to talk in the hospital. Will he be angry?

At least I'm running. It's nearly eight and the morning light is spreading all silvery over the sea. I've done my paper route and I'm jogging across the soft sand around the yacht club and my legs are sinking in, my calf muscles aching like mad because they're so out of practice. I've got to get back into training before the marathon coach kicks me off the squad. Trudy is running beside me, her ears flopping back and forth, her big pink tongue hanging out of her mouth. She started to yelp with joy as soon as we set off from the cottage. It's ages since we've had a good run.

Around the point, the beach is very narrow and more pebbly but I try to keep my pace up as I head toward the Lifeboat Station. It still feels weird to think of our hut empty, and I had to stop myself from filling the hot-water bottle for Mohammed this morning when I got up. It makes me feel all shivery when I think how close he came to being discovered. How close we all came. Mrs. Saddler definitely had her suspicions but it was all over before she could really nose around. She seems to think I've been up to something good, not bad, at least. Unlike Mum and Dad.

Will Dad show up for bowling on Saturday morning? Not if the Gremlin has anything to do with it! That thought makes me feel so mad, I sprint all the way home.

When I get in there's an amazing smell of frying coming from the kitchen. I rush upstairs, change for school, scoot back down to the kitchen and Mum puts a plate of bacon, egg, beans, fried bread, toast and tea in front of me. She's even balancing on her crutches like a circus act.

"Leave the stuff in the sink," I say through a mouthful of toast. "I'll clean up when I get home."

"No you won't," she says, and she's got a dishcloth in her hand. "Time I pulled my weight around here."

So she really means it, I think as I collect my backpack and saunter off down to the bus stop, early for once.

School is the pits. Everyone is talking about the stabbing and what Samir must have done to wind Terrence Bellows up.

"I heard he nicked Terrence's skunk," Charlie Parks is saying as I walk into class.

"Two Percent hasn't got it in him," sneers Lindy, and the Jayne family all laugh.

"So is he dead?" says Jess in a bored voice.

"My dad says they're all scroungers," sneers Charlie. "He's probably faking it, so he gets the rest of the week off school."

I feel myself getting really angry and I look around the class for Kim. But then I remember she and Steven have orchestra practice all morning. I turn back to Jess and the others and I'm about to speak when Mr. Spicer comes in and yells at us to sit down.

He spots me and says, "You missed your detention, Alix. You'll do an hour tonight. Ring your mother to say you'll be late." Hoots of laughter whip around the classroom. Doesn't anyone care about what has happened?

Then he says something about the principal calling a parents' meeting after school next week about the stabbing. "You'll get letters on Monday and I want you all there."

No way, I think, no one seems to care about Samir, so why should I go?

I manage to snatch five minutes with Kim at lunchtime and then she has to go off to a dental appointment. The afternoon really drags by and then I have to meet Spicer back in the form room for detention.

He looks up when I come in, "Any news of Samir?"

"I don't know, sir," I say. "But I'm going around to the hospital later." I don't know if I'll be allowed to see him but maybe Spicer will let me off early.

"Good, give him my regards," says Spicer, "you've got an hour. Do the next twenty questions."

Weasel!

I don't escape until five and I race across town to the hospital. But they won't let me onto the ward.

"Samir banged his head when he fell," explains the nurse. "He's not up to visitors."

"What about the stab wound?" I ask anxiously.

"It was quite deep but there's no damage to the organs. Come back after the weekend, dear."

How can I wait that long?

Then my phone goes. It's Pritesh.

"No cell phones," says the nurse, and I run downstairs and just get outside before the phone stops ringing.

"What's happened? Where's Mohammed?" I ask, panting. "Don't worry, everything's fine," says Pritesh. "The lawyer has been in touch with the Home Office and it's been agreed that Mohammed can apply for asylum. So he won't be deported, at least not for now."

I'm shaking with relief and I tell him we'll come and see Mohammed as soon as Samir's better.

All I want to do is rush back into the hospital and tell Samir, but I'll never get past the nurses. In the end I tear a page out of my math book and write Samir a note.

EvERYONE is safe. Get better soon. Alix x

The nurse promises to give it to Samir but all the way home I'm worrying about that *x*. What if Naazim sees it? Are Muslims allowed to write *x*?

Friday goes by in a blur of math tests and worrying about Samir. But finally it's Saturday morning and Dad and I are at the bowling alley.

He's doing his best, saying, "Pull up your pants, Alix" and "How about a cookie, doll?" but things just feel weird.

It's been two years since we did stuff together. One seventh of my entire life.

And then I get a strike.

"Way to go, doll," yells Dad, and we do a high five and things feel a bit more normal.

So I say, "Does the..." and I'm about to say Gremlin but manage to stop just in time, "...er, Gloria, does she know where you are?"

"Sure," says Dad with this glittery smile but I don't believe him.

"Mum says she doesn't like kids. Is that why you didn't stay in touch?"

Dad's quiet for a minute and there's the bumping sound of the bowling balls rolling back down the tunnel and some little kid whining for sweets.

Then he says, "We talked about it and Gloria felt that if I kept in touch it would be harder for you. All that coming and going. So we agreed I would make a clean break. Your mum didn't want me to keep in touch either."

They're all as bad as each other, I decide.

"But Gloria really wants to meet you," he goes on in this sort of eager voice. "She's great, Gloria, she manages a little boutique in Southampton, knows all the latest fashions," and he's looking at me hopefully.

"Yeah, right," I say in a scornful voice, and I can tell he's disappointed even though I avoid his eyes. I turn away and roll my ball straight down the gutter.

Our game is over so we get some burgers and eat in silence and I'm thinking, He's sorry he came back. He thinks I'm just a worthless teenager, with a bad attitude. He's probably relieved he doesn't have to introduce the Daughter from Hell to his girl-friend. I glance up at him but his eyes are on his cell phone, tapping out a message. He can't wait to get back to her, I decide. I'm not going bowling ever again.

Then he says, "I lost my job yesterday."

Here we go, I think, and I push my chair back. Might as well leave now before he gives out all the usual excuses.

But he reaches up and grabs my arm and says quickly, "No, wait, Alix. Hear me out, please."

So I slump back down in the chair and say sullenly, "You've got one minute." I start to tear up the greasy burger box into lit-tle pieces, flicking them off the table as I go. The floor's getting in a right mess but I don't care.

"It was all my fault," he says quietly.

"You what?" I wasn't expecting that. He usually blames someone else when he loses his job. I stop tearing up the burger box.

"I was late three times on deliveries because I didn't use the GPS properly," he explains. I'm looking at him and his face is very close to mine. He has this sort of serious, intense look I've never seen before.

"But I'm going to get another job straightaway, Alix, and you know why?"

I shake my head and we're so close my hair flicks over his forehead but he doesn't move away.

"Because of you."

"What do you mean?"

And we're sort of whispering as if we're afraid to talk too loud in case this moment just disappears.

"Because you need things for school, and outings to the bowling alley with me and American DVDs to keep up your vocabulary."

He stops and I'm staring right into his eyes, which are brown like mine, and he's not even blinking, like Kim does when she wants to mesmerize. I want us to stay like this forever. Because he's chosen me. Not Mum and definitely not Gloria, his girlfriend, the Gremlin. He's chosen to get a new job because of me!

He wants to go bowling with me and buy me stuff like other dads and it feels like there's a hopeful little frog jumping about inside me.

I can't help grinning and then he tilts his head forward and kisses me on the cheek. That feels good.

Let's hope he means what he says for once.

38. No Regrets

It rains all day Monday. Kim sits sneezing in class next to me until finally the teachers send her home. We only just have time for me to fill her in about Mohammed.

"He's safe, Ali, isn't that a relief? And no one guessed, it's quite funny really. Once Samir's better we should have a party. My sister'll get some cans for us."

"Muslims don't drink," I tell her, but it feels good to be laughing about something again.

After school I decide to go around to the hospital and insist on seeing Samir but when I get there they tell me he's been discharged. I'm not sure what to do next. I don't have his phone number and Naazim probably won't let me in. But Samir might not be back at school for weeks. I just can't wait that long.

So I take my chances and go around to Samir's flat. When I get there I ring the doorbell. The Chinese lady from the takeout comes out and looks me up and down slowly.

"Too late," she says. "He not want girlfriend now." She kicks a bit of rubbish into the gutter and goes back into her shop.

I can hear someone coming downstairs slowly and then Auntie Selma opens the door and throws her arms around me. "Alix, *habibti*, darling, come, come."

We go upstairs and into the kitchen and Naazim is there with his back to me, swilling something around in the sink.

Samir is sitting at the table and I stand there thinking, Should I give him a hug like Kim and Steven always do? But I'm pretty certain Naazim would throw me out so I just say, "Hi."

"Hi," says Samir, and he gets up.

He's looking really different and then I realize he's wearing new clothes. He's got a new blue sweatshirt on with Lions of Mesopotamia on it—where did he get that?—and new jeans, and when I look down at his feet, he's wearing brand-new Nike sneakers.

"You look cool," I say.

"Naazim got them for me," he says with a shy smile. "He had the shirt made specially."

Naazim is fiddling around with the cutlery and I'm expecting him to say something like, "English football's rubbish," or something else mean but he stays silent.

Auntie Selma insists I stay to dinner, which I have to admit isn't my favorite idea as Naazim's sitting about six inches from my nose. It's a very small kitchen.

She's cooked up a storm and she piles our plates high with rice and chicken and *foul,* which are like big brown beans in a thick sauce.

I'm too nervous to eat and Auntie Selma is laughing and saying, "Plenty rice, Alix, eat," and she's pushing my plate toward me but I'm just waiting for Naazim to kick off. I know he's going to blame me for everything.

And then he starts to speak.

"Samir has said to me everything on Mohammed."

Oh God, I think. Now there'll be fireworks. I stare across at Samir and for once I'm the one pleading with my eyes. But he isn't looking at me. He's glued to his brother and he doesn't even look worried. Maybe Naazim has turned him against me.

I suddenly feel like crying because that would be so unfair. It wasn't even my idea in the first place to hide Mohammed. Not that I regret it now. Whatever Naazim says, I know we did the right thing.

"I can't believe what you and my brother have did," Naazim goes on.

His eyes are drilling into mine. I think, What if he hits me? I'm sure he's got a real temper and he's been a soldier. He's probably killed people; slapping a fourteen-year-old girl is nothing. Why don't I ever have anyone on my side?

I can't hold the tears back any longer. I feel so stupid as they run down my face and I try to brush them away. But they just keep pouring down.

Then Naazim speaks again, only in a really quiet, gentle voice, "No, please don't to cry. You did a good thing, Alix. A very good thing."

"Very good, *habibti*," nods Auntie Selma, piling more rice onto my plate.

"You give to me and my family something very special," Naazim goes on.

Have I just landed on a different planet? I can't believe this. I try to catch Samir's eye but he's swirling his fork around in his rice.

Naazim is struggling with his English and he mutters something in Arabic to Samir, which sounds like "leisure" and Samir says, "Refugee."

"Yes, refugee, we are refugee. I come to this country when I sixteen. Nobody care. Nobody help us or talk to us," says Naazim. He's leaning toward me as he talks in this urgent voice as if it's really important I understand him.

"My little brother he is all alone, he is sad boy. No mummy, no daddy, I am mummy and daddy now."

"*Inshallah*," says Aunty Selma.

Naazim suddenly looks so young and vulnerable, like you could just push him over, and he's nineteen, way older than me.

"You are the first one to make us feel somebody care," he goes on. "You hide Mohammed and you don't tell nobody. You make us feel somebody want refugee for the first time since we run away from Iraq." He looks down at his plate and shrugs. "I don't know nothing more to say."

It goes very quiet in the kitchen except for Auntie Selma running the water in the sink, which is soothing, and I suddenly realize how I misjudged Naazim. He's not mean at all, just very protective of his brother and weighed down with too much responsibility.

Well, I know what that feels like.

Samir wants me to tell them all about Mohammed and when I've finished he says, "That's just what I would have done." Then he leans over and gives me a kiss on the cheek.

I go bright red and glance at Naazim. He doesn't meet my eyes but he doesn't say anything either. For a few seconds the room is very quiet, just the sound of a tap dripping in the sink and the Chinese lady calling out in the shop below.

Then Samir gives a loud burp and I look over in surprise. He says, "In Iraq it is a compliment to the cook to burp."

"Zank you," says Auntie Selma, and her face splits in a huge grin.

"*Shukran*, Auntie Selma," I say. "Thank you very much."

Everyone laughs, even Naazim, and starts to shout in Arabic and English and pass the food around again.

39. Out of Hiding

Samir has to take all the next week off school to recover and it feels so empty every day without him sitting at the back of the class. There's so much to catch up on I don't even have time to go around after school. I ring him and say I'll definitely come over on Saturday. Hopefully Naazim will still be friendly.

I'm way behind in my course work so I spend all my lunch-times in the library and after school I'm back in training. The marathon coach is giving me another chance. Kim is practicing hard for the orchestra too so we hardly see each other.

Every evening, however cold it is, me and Trudy are on the beach. When I'm running by the water and the shrouds are jangling on the boats and the tide is swishing over the pebbles, I forget about everything else—Mum, Dad, Mohammed, the smugglers and the racist bullies. It's only alone in my bedroom at night listening to the foghorns in the dark that I remember Samir's face as he dropped to the ground, the blood, Terrence's ugly laugh.

When I get home from school on Thursday there's a strange car parked outside the house with a huge striped drinks can sticking out the roof. I let myself in and Mum appears in the living room doorway.

"We're going out in half an hour, I've made some tea."

I look at her blankly. "Out? Where? I've got homework and marathon training."

I follow her into the living room.

Dad is sitting on the sofa with Trudy on his lap. "Hey, doll," he says with a big grin. "How's your friend Samir?"

Mum is fussing around pouring tea and cutting cake. I sit down and say, "He's getting better. So what's going on?"

"It's the meeting tonight," says Mum, and she's holding up a letter from school. She must have fished it out of the trash. The principal called a meeting of Year 10 and their parents because everyone was so upset about the stabbing. Well, the parents were. Me and Kim had decided to go on our own. We didn't want any more fuss at home.

"Oh, that," I say with a shrug. "Didn't think you'd be interested."

"We're all going together, Alix, as a family, and before you say anything else," Dad puts his hand up as I open my mouth to protest, "Kim is going with her family too. I've spoken to her dad."

"You what?" I can't believe it. And Mum's going through the trash for school letters. That's what proper parents do, isn't it? I'm almost impressed.

Trudy pushes her nose into my hand and I pet her for a minute and then I say, "Well, we've missed the bus and there isn't another one for ages."

"Your dad's giving us a lift," says Mum, and Dad grins and goes over to the window. I follow him and stare out. He's pointing to the car with the can sticking out the roof.

"Got new wheels, doll. What do you think?"

He can't be serious. "I'm not pulling up to school in *that*. I'd never hear the end of it. Where did you get it?"

"My new job. I collect the money from vending machines," says Dad.

It's a real squash in the car and Mum moans all the way because the heater doesn't work. I'm more worried about arriving at school at the same time as the Jayne family. I can just imagine Jess Jayne screeching, "Left the Merc behind, did you?"

Kim sends me a text as we cross the bridge, *Savd u a seat r u stll cming?*

Do I have a choice? I wonder as I text back, *Yes.* It feels weird that Mum and Dad are doing stuff together again, and for me as well. I'm sort of happy, I just wish they hadn't started with this stupid meeting.

When we get to the school hall I leave Mum and Dad with the other parents and go and sit next to Kim.

"This was one secret we didn't manage to keep," she says.

"At least it was only a letter they found and not the hut," I say, and Kim's eyes widen as she nods.

Then the principal taps on the microphone. It crackles and he asks everyone to sit down. There's a lot of shoving and giggling as people huddle up with their friends.

The Jayne family dump themselves down in the back row and I can see them talking behind their hands and nodding at me. Lindy is here too, sitting on the end of a row, surreptitiously drinking what looks like a can of beer. Steven and his geeky Science Club are lined up in the front row and they all seem to be taking notes.

The principal is about to speak when I hear Lindy call out, "Where's Two Percent?"

I can't believe it. I crane around and catch her eye but she looks away. At least she doesn't carry on yelling out, which is a relief. Then the principal calls for silence and the Jayne family cackle behind their hands like witches. Charlie Parks and a couple of his football mates are sitting behind me and Kim, kicking our chairs. What if they decide to turn this into a riot? There's only a couple of teachers here with the principal. I imagine things getting out of control and those two policemen who were sniffing around the beach for illegal immigrants, Good Cop and Bad Cop, turning up with plastic shields to clear the room.

The principal starts to speak and he's saying all the stuff the parents want to hear about how the school is a tolerant school, where everyone is welcome and treated equally.

Kim and I exchange looks and I feel sick and angry. I'm almost ready to walk out. Nothing's changed, can't he see that? I lean over to whisper this to Kim as the principal wraps up his speech, but then he looks over to the side of the stage and gives a nod to someone.

It's Samir! He walks over to the microphone and he's still a bit bent over to the side from his wound. He looks very small on the stage next to the principal, who's a former rugby international. What on earth is going on?

A mutter goes up around the hall and Charlie Parks whispers, "Taliban." There's a horrible sniggering behind me and I clench my fists.

Samir has a small piece of paper in his hands and he begins reading in a slow, hesitant voice, "I was sent out of Iraq when I was nine years old because it was too dangerous to stay there. When I arrived in England they called me 'asylum seeker' ... and sometimes 'terrorist.'"

There are more mutterings and whisperings behind me and I can hear Charlie Parks giggling and saying something down his row. Why don't they just shut up and listen?

The principal looks around the hall, frowning, and someone

from the Science Club says, "You're all right, mate." Someone else behind says, "Just ignore them."

I twist around to catch Mum's eye. She gives me a firm nod and Dad grins. Maybe it's a good thing they're here. I turn back, feeling calmer. This is going to be okay, I'm thinking. Not everyone agrees with Charlie and his mates.

Samir carries on and his voice is a bit stronger now. "They put me in a foster home and I was very lonely but a year later my brother and my auntie arrived and we made a new family in England..."

I'm thinking, Tell them how you're in all the top sets even though you have to help your auntie make pastries to sell to make ends meet. I almost call out, but I don't.

But then the shuffling and rustling starts up behind me again. I can't concentrate on what Samir is saying. I turn around to tell them to shut up and Charlie is holding up a piece of paper. He has a horrible sneer on his face. I catch a glimpse—it's a drawing. It looks like it's meant to be a suicide bomber.

"Give me that," I hiss at Charlie, and the muttering gets louder around me. The principal calls out for silence. I try to catch Samir's eye but he's looking at his shoes. Oh God, what if he thinks I'm against him as well?

Then Samir looks up, and he's staring out at the hall, frozen into the ice man again. His hand is holding the left side of his body where the knife went in. I feel really angry that the principal has made him do this. He glances to the end of a row and I follow his eyes. Naazim and Auntie Selma are sitting there, and Naazim is nodding to Samir. I think how alike they are, the brothers, watching out for each other against the odds.

I catch Samir's eye at last and give him an encouraging smile and the thumbs-up. So he takes a deep breath and starts reading from his paper again. "But I am very happy now in England. I want to study hard and go to college..."

Suddenly a paper airplane soars through the air. It bumps into his chest and settles on his own piece of paper. "Bull's-eye!" someone shouts, and a smattering of laughter whips around the hall. Samir opens the paper and his head goes down. I know it's Charlie's picture.

I'm so angry my blood's gone way beyond boiling point and bright colors are dancing in front of my eyes.

Kim's arm is already reaching for me but it's too late.

I throw myself to my feet and I want to yell out, "Racist pigs!" But I just stand there like an idiot with everyone staring at me, and it feels like all the breath has gone out of my body. I can't change the world all by myself, can I? I'm not a leader like Jess Jayne or Charlie Parks.

The muttering spreads around the hall and Kim's hand is on my arm, tugging at me to sit down. Then I feel it. Welling inside me like a tsunami, sweeping me forward in a giant wave of rage. I know exactly what I have to do.

"Who runs this school?" I bellow, and I almost tip over with the effort. "Them," I shout, pointing to Charlie and his mates, "or us? Do we have to do everything those stupid idiots do? Me and my friends don't agree with them," and there's a murmur of agreement from around me. "Who's brave enough to join us and show those bullies what we really think of them?"

For a second there is silence as the words hang in the air, glittering like sunlight on the sea. This is the moment, I think, don't hide away anymore.

"You should listen to Samir," I go on. "It's amazing what he and his family have done. I've never heard anything like it, and neither have you. They had to be so brave to run away from their homeland and try and start a new life in England. Imagine if you had to go and live in Iraq."

A bit of a gasp went up around the hall. They're probably thinking of all those bombs. I can't stop now, can I? "We sit in our safe little houses and walk on our safe little beaches while there are people suffering and dying and being beheaded in their own homes. People like you and me and our families, schoolkids and mums and dads and grannies and babies and, and..." I run out of steam and I just stand there looking down at everyone staring up at me.

For a moment it's like when the tide turns in the bay, sucking back across the beach, revealing all the hidden mudflats and driftwood and washed-up treasures from thousands of miles away. There's nowhere left for me to hide now and I don't know which way they'll swing but I've made my decision against the tide.

A small voice rings out beside me, "I'm with Alix." It's Kim.

A couple of the boys in the Science Club call out, "Me too!"

There are some grumbles as well but something shifts around the hall.

Then suddenly a huge, "YESS!!" bursts out from the Science Club and they do a Mexican wave down their row. It's a bit daft but then everyone is clapping and even a few cheers break out.

I catch Lindy's eye and she gives me a slight nod. Even the Jayne family are paying attention, gasping and looking at each other, astonished.

I look at the stage and Samir's head has gone up and he's looking at me with the full monty smile wide across his face. He lifts up his paper and the hall falls silent as though with a new respect.

He starts to read again but now his voice is strong and confident. "I had to leave Iraq in 2002 because my parents were tortured and murdered by Saddam Hussein." A gasp goes out around the hall. "But now my brother and I are safe." He pauses and then he says in a clear voice, "In Iraq, my parents wanted me to be a doctor and now I'm here, that's what I want too."

I breathe a sigh of relief and drop back into my chair as Kim gives me a big hug.

The principal walks over to Samir and shakes his hand and Samir is smiling and nodding and then Naazim leaps up onto the stage and shakes the principal's hand too.

So it's not just Mohammed who came out of hiding this week.

Samir, the ice man, has shattered into tiny pieces. There's no way he'll let the bullies crush him anymore.

And me? I'm riding my elephant through the school hall, standing up against the rising tide, just like Grandpa did in his war.

His words echo in my ear. "If you're fourteen and strong enough, Alix, you can do anything."

I look around at Mum and Dad and remember Dad's promise to stay in touch and how Mum's started to do stuff around the house again. It feels as though a big weight has fallen off my shoulders and I'm floating above them, looking down from a great height.

I'll steer my own course from now on and they'll just have to keep up with me!

About Miriam Halahmy

I am married and have two grown-up children and a grandchild and I live in London. On my father's side I am only second-generation British. My grandparents came from Poland before WWI, escaping pogroms against the Jews, and my mother's family came for the same reason in the nineteenth century. England gave my ancestors a home and a future in a time of great need.

My husband was born in Baghdad into an Iraqi Jewish family. The entire Jewish community of Iraq were forced into exile in the 1950s, and most went to Israel where they lived in refugee camps, sometimes for years. The stories the Halahmy family told about Baghdad brought alive for me the markets and streets; the food and the pigeon keepers; the fishermen who grilled fish down by the river Tigris and how people slept on the roof in summer. The family still has one foot back in the Arabic world. Their stories helped me to create the Iraqi characters in my book and the world they came from that they miss so much.

I was a teacher in London for twenty-five years and worked with children from all over the world, many of whom were asylum seekers. But I have written since childhood and have published novels, short stories and poetry for children, teens and adults. My writing focuses on realistic stories with ordinary characters facing extraordinary situations and digging deep to find the hero in themselves.

One of the most important issues of the 21st century is the plight of refugees and how the world responds to their needs and aspirations. I have led writing workshops for asylum seekers through English PEN and the Medical Foundation for the Victims of Torture to help them write down their stories and come to terms with their lives.

My experiences both from my family background and my work have given me insight into this group in society. The inspiration behind the writing of *Hidden* was a desire to show that each asylum seeker is an individual just like you and me.

I have been active since I was a teenager promoting peace, tolerance and diversity. I believe that all divided communities can build bridges and all societies can embrace diversity if they wish. We should be prepared to stand up to any injustice, however small. All young people have a future, and reading can offer a map forward.